GAME FOR DEMONS

GAME
FOR
DEMONS

by

Ben Shecter

Harper & Row, Publishers
New York, Evanston,
San Francisco, London

GAME FOR DEMONS

Copyright © 1972 by Ben Shecter

Library of Congress Catalog Card Number: 72-80369
Trade Standard Book Number: 06-025578-1
Harpercrest Standard Book Number: 06-025579-X

FIRST EDITION

For my mother

Contents

GAME FOR DEMONS

I

MOTHER'S DECISION

Sometimes I pretend I'm a werewolf. It just happens at different times, and I sure felt like giving out with a long, low howl while I waited for my mother to make up her mind about the summer bungalow.

I couldn't understand why my mother made such a fuss when Mr. Steiner told her she couldn't have the same bungalow we had the summer before.

First of all, she was late in making up her mind about returning to the shore. Second of all, all the bungalows were exactly the same inside and out. But most of all, Mother had said over and over again on the train ride out that she had a feeling we wouldn't be getting the same bungalow again.

And when my mother got a feeling she was

usually right. Like the time she said she had a feeling I was going to rip the pants of my new suit, and I did. Then there was the time she told my sister Myra that if she didn't put her house key on a ring she would lose it. And that afternoon when the doorbell rang, my mother said, "That's Myra—she lost her key." And my mother was right again.

I felt like walking away and I'm sure my father and Myra did too, when my mother started raising her voice to Mr. Steiner.

She said things like, "It's the principle of the thing," and "I just put new shelving paper down the week before we left."

Mr. Steiner just held out his hands and kept saying, "I'm sorry, Mrs. Cassman, but it's rented."

When my mother said that she would talk to the people about exchanging bungalows, Mr. Steiner finally raised his voice and said, "Take it or leave it." I wanted her to say yes, because I really hated the Bronx in the summertime. Most of the kids in the neighborhood just sat around and did nothing.

Clapping her hands together, mother spoke half to my father and half to Mr. Steiner. "Of all bungalows," she said, "it would be the one that belonged to that crazy Widow Kravitz."

And my father, who was an unusually patient

2

man, spoke up. "Betty," he said—that's my mother's name—"you either want it or you don't."

My mother gave my father a dirty look and kept quiet for a while. Then she sat down on the bungalow porch and rocked herself in a beat-up old rocking chair.

I couldn't understand why my father wanted this whole bungalow thing in the first place. He spent so much time traveling back and forth on the train, he was just too tired at the end of the day to spend any time with us. "Mr. Steiner is waiting for a decision, dear," he said, I guess feeling about as uncomfortable as me by the long silence. I know he added the "dear" to avoid another dirty look but he got one all the same.

The rocking chair was really getting a workout from my mother. Then she got up and looked in the bungalow window, and when she sat down again I could see on her face that something was bothering her. I sort of knew what it was, and I began to push it out of my head by watching Myra pull the petals off of a plastic rose. But that wasn't even any good, because instead of playing "She loves me, she loves me not" to myself, I began to say, "I will live, I will die." Before Myra got to the last few petals I looked up and watched some swooping gulls.

3

Usually I'm very good about purposely forgetting things. When I see a real scary movie, if I think hard enough I can just put it out of my head. And that's what I did with Widow Kravitz. Up until now.

Widow Kravitz was very religious and went to synagogue every Saturday, and it was really far. She'd walk there at times when it was so hot no one even felt like going to the beach. Everyone laughed about it. My mother even said, "God would forgive her if she missed one Saturday."

I once looked in her window and saw her without her wig and without her teeth, and she looked scary. I told all the kids about it, and Larry Perl began to call her Monster Lady. And from that time on everyone began to call her Monster Lady.

She didn't bother with anyone, and she was real old, and sometimes she'd complain about the noise we'd make.

Well, one time we painted a swastika on her door, and she got real mad and hollered something about us all going to suffer.

When my mother heard about it she got upset, and for some reason it bothered her enough to go over and try to talk nice to Widow Kravitz. But she didn't even let my mother in. Boy, was I sorry I ever told anyone what I had seen through the window.

4

Myra whispered something to my mother and went inside the bungalow. "Make sure it's clean," Mother yelled out after her.

It seemed that girls were always going to the bathroom. And I know it wasn't just my sister Myra, because the girls at school were always leaving the room also.

"Gordie, do you have to use the facilities?" my mother said.

Sometimes my mother really knocks me out with the things she comes out with. All the time she says bathroom—now in front of Mr. Steiner she tries to be fancy. I really wanted to say, "No, I don't have to pee," and ruin her, but most of the time I never really say what I'm thinking.

Sometimes I think my name is phony, like it wasn't for me. It seems like it was given to me to impress people. My mother named me after Gordon MacRae, the movie actor-singer, who my mother thinks is the greatest. I suppose she thought I'd grow up to be a singer too. Boy, it would also ruin her if she knew that I was class listener since second grade.

I could hear the toilet flush, and when Myra came out it was like some signal for things to begin again. My mother looked at me and Myra, and still with a

5

troubled look on her face she shook her head yes. "Okay, we'll take it," she said.

Mr. Steiner looked like he was about to faint, and my father had a thank-God-it's-over look on his face (a look I'd seen so many times after my mother stopped yelling about something). Myra said, "Good!" I knew why she was happy. It meant seeing her dopey boyfriend, Irwin Friedman, from last summer again.

"Now that's settled," said my father. "Let's eat." It was my father who always suggested we eat. I suppose it must have something to do with his being a waiter.

My mother hardly ate anything, and she kept saying, "I hope we did the right thing."

For the next few days everything smelled like mothballs. Myra and me had to help take stuff down and put stuff away. I laughed when Myra tried on her bathing suit. Myra was really getting big, and on top, too.

I guess next to my birthday the last day of school is just about the best day of the year. All the kids just sit around and play games and talk. When I told them I was going back to the shore again they said I was a lucky stiff. When the three o'clock bell rang that day we all ran out of the school screaming.

It was a good chance for me to give out with a howl. Everyone thought I howled better than the werewolf in the movies. The night before we left for the shore, Myra wrote some things in her diary, and I'm sure it was things about Irwin Friedman. Myra's big on secrets. She always hides her diary. As if I care what she wrote in that dumb book. My sister Myra is funny. It's like she's made up of lots of secrets. It's all right. She never tells me hers, so I never tell her mine.

Myra and me sometimes play who can outstare each other. And when that happens she stares like she can look right through you. When you look hard into her eyes you can see that they're sort of yellow-green. I have green eyes too, but they never change color like hers do. Whenever Myra starts to get the best of me in the staring game, I become a werewolf. No one can outstare Myra.

On the morning we were getting ready to leave, my mother broke the sugar jar. She got really shook, because my mother never breaks anything. While she was cleaning it up she whispered to herself, but loud enough for me and Myra to hear, "I've got a feeling and it's not so good."

Myra and me looked at each other. Suddenly I got a case of the goose bumps.

I had the same feeling but I didn't say anything.

7

2

THUNDERSHOWERS

The sun was out when we left for the shore, and I made a bet with Myra that I was going to beat her to the beach. But when we got off the train the sun was gone. It looked like it was going to rain. I don't mind when it rains, I just hate in-between days. It was a card-playing kind of day like I remembered from the summer before. Myra was good at cards, and she never cheated. She taught me most of the games I know. Larry Perl taught me strip poker, but when I wanted to teach it to Myra she said it was obscene.

I knew a shortcut from the station to the bunga-low. I'm great at shortcuts. I discovered this one from all the times I went to the station last summer to wait for my father. He'd come down every night after work. I tried to tell my mother and Myra to come my way. But my mother said we'd probably end up getting lost. My mother is really chicken about trying new things, like when I invent different kinds of omelettes. I'll admit some of them aren't the greatest, but my banana-and-chocolate is really sensational, and she won't even try it.

Having to go the long way really made me mad, especially since I was carrying two suitcases that weren't exactly filled with feathers. My mother really knows how to load up a suitcase. Myra carried some shopping bags. Mother carried suitcases and shopping bags. And there were more suitcases waiting for my father when he came after work. We kept stopping for Myra, who said her hands were falling off. My arms were breaking also. Like I'm no Hercules—a lot of people kid me about being too skinny. My mother finally dropped everything she was carrying and sat on a suitcase.

"We should have stayed home and bought an air-conditioner," my mother complained while fanning herself with her hand. As if that did any good.

"We should have taken the shortcut," I said, trying to rub it in. Sometimes I really like to rub it in, especially when someone thinks they know better than I do, and then they find out that I was right in the first place.

Steiner's Sunshine Bungalows were stuck between Stutman's Rooming House and the Breeze Front Hotel. The name Sunshine Bungalows was a come-on because the sun never really got to them. Stutman's and the Breeze Front were both big wooden buildings with lots of porches around them, and they blocked out all the sun from Steiner's.

Last summer Larry Perl dared me to jump off from a high porch at Stutman's, and I did it too. I was pretty scared, but I did it because I didn't want Larry to think I was scared, and anyway, if I didn't do it he'd end up calling me fag all summer. That's how Larry was—if you didn't do what he wanted he'd end up calling you some dumb name and then all the kids would start calling you that too.

Larry was older than me, almost the same age as Myra, and I guess it was a big deal that he let me hang around with him. Larry did lots of things that weren't so hot. It was his idea about the swastika on Widow Kravitz's door. I have to admit Larry knew a lot about sex things. The more I thought about Larry, the more I began to wonder if we would hang around together this summer.

"Are you children hungry?" asked my mother. "I have sandwiches with me."

When Myra and me told her we weren't, she went into this long thing about later when we are, we'll be sorry we didn't eat now. I was beginning to think my mother wasn't in such a hurry about getting to the bungalow.

We walked in and out of sandy paths around the bungalows. Some of the seashell boundaries from the summer before were still there. All the time we kept ducking under clotheslines. Mrs. Friedman, who was on her front porch beating the daylights out of a blanket, yelled, "Hello!"

"I'm still getting the sand out from last summer," she said.

"Don't remind me," said my mother, who stopped to talk. Now my mother is a big talker, but when Mrs. Friedman gets started she makes my mother seem like a lockjaw case. And it seemed to me like another stall.

Myra tried to look inside the bungalow to see if Irwin was there. Mrs. Friedman caught Myra's action, and she said, "My Irwin's a lifeguard this summer at the Blue Channel Day Camp." She said it like being a lifeguard was some big deal.

"It's funny about you getting Widow Kravitz's place," said Mrs. Friedman. "Do you know that she stayed on past Labor Day? I know, because when we left she was still here."

My mother looked around before she spoke again. "I'd hate to stay here by myself." She wiped her forehead with one of the millions of tissues she carries. "You could die here and no one would know it."

Mother's comment reminded me about there not being any phones in the bungalow, and when you wanted to make a call you had to go to Markey's Appetizing Store where the phone always smelled liked pickled herring.

We started on our way again, and passed the bungalow we had the year before. Only a few shells remained of the big star I made in front. A wheelchair was on the porch.

"I wonder who has the place this year," said mother. I knew one thing. Whoever belonged to the chair was either old or sick or both.

"They should thank me a thousand times for leaving them such a clean place," said my mother.

"It must be awful being confined to a wheelchair," said Myra.

"Oh, I don't know," I said. "It beats walking, especially when you don't take shortcuts."

"Bite your tongue!" said my mother. If I bit my tongue all the times my mother told me to, I wouldn't have a tongue left. Whenever I say something about putting myself in a bad situation, my mother always says, "Bite your tongue." She said it when I told her some kids in my class were lucky to be out of school because they had the measles. My mother has lots of superstitions and for some reason I half believe them.

I began to picture myself in a wheelchair, and the more I thought about it the more scared I got. I scare myself when I see blind people. I get a terrible feeling like I'm going to go blind.

As we reached the bungalow it began to thunder. "Just in time!" said Myra, who I think was really afraid of thunder and lightning but wouldn't admit to it. Mother was at the tissues again, wiping her face. "Well, we're here!" She said it like after ironing a heavy load of laundry.

Inside the bungalow it was almost wet, and cool and dark, like when you go into a cellar. I remember the bungalow last year was hot and stuffy. I half-closed my eyes and everything disappeared into a gray-brown color. It seemed as if the room had been closed for a very long time—I mean like longer than just a winter season.

"What that poor woman must have gone through," said Myra. I knew what Myra was talking about and I felt awful.

"She was a crazy lady," said Mother, who I knew was really trying to wipe the whole thing out of her head. Myra was a real softie anyway—like she cried over dead birds that she didn't know, and she said she wanted to be a nurse so that she could help all the sick people of the world. Sometimes I think Myra got really corny, but I knew how she felt about some things. Because I felt the same way about animals. But I never thought about the sick people of the world.

"It's dark in here, Gordie, put the light on. This place needs a good cleaning," said Mother, who had barely dropped her suitcases. "Gordie, this will be your room." My room was the all-purpose kitchen-living room that looked like it was put together with tossed-out furniture. My bed was to be a lumpy cot disguised as a sofa that sagged in the middle.

Myra got her own room. It was really more like a big closet, but anyway it was private. And the first thing she did was find a secret place for her diary. There were a few more big grumbles outside and flashes of light, and then I heard the rain hitting the roof.

"Gordie, you'll have to get shelving paper," said Mother, who was already on a chair looking in the closet.

"I can't go—it's raining," I said. "Anyway, why doesn't Myra go?"

We always have this big thing about who should go to the store, me or Myra. I always end up going because Myra's always just finished either washing, drying or setting her hair.

"Look what I found!" said my mother holding a lady's hat in her hands. I recognized it right away. It was the hat Widow Kravitz wore to synagogue every Saturday.

"Her Shabbos hat," said my mother, who looked upset and puzzled. "Why would she leave a thing like that?"

3

PAINTED SNEAKERS

"WoooooooWoooooooAHWooooooo!" I heard a howl on the porch and looked up. I really didn't have to look up to know who it was. It was Larry Perl, and he pushed his face up against the screen door, making a big bump in it. Larry was trying to imitate me. All last summer he tried to do it, but he couldn't. I knew Larry thought his howl was really great, because when one of the kids told him that I do it better he said all he was trying to do was to show how dumb the whole thing was in the first place. But I think he was just full of bull when he said that.

His howl changed to a crazy laugh. "Is Wolfman at home?" he asked.

My mother got to the door before me. "Larry Perl!" she laughed. "What are you doing out in the rain?" It figured for Larry to be out in the rain, because that's how he was. Larry had a rain hat pulled over his eyes, and his sneakers were painted with Stars of David and weird designs I didn't recognize.

He gave my mother a big "Hello!" and asked her how she was feeling. Larry was the kind of guy if he wanted to he could make all mothers think he was the greatest, and say to their own kids, "Now why aren't you like Larry Perl?"

"How're ya doin', Gordie?" Larry said in a phony Western accent. He turned up the brim of his hat.

"Hi, Larry," I said. Then I got the kind of feeling I get when I meet someone for the first time. Like it all doesn't seem natural at first, and until it does there seems to be an uncomfortable, long stretch of time. And anyway some of the bad memories from the end of last summer didn't make things easier.

"Howdy, Myra," said Larry still with the dumb Western accent.

Myra said, "Hello," and vanished into her room. Either Myra was trying to be real cool or else she didn't like Larry, or maybe both.

17

Larry winked and smiled a crooked smile like the gambler always does in a cowboy saloon before he accuses someone of cheating and then shoots him from under the table. Larry was also big on different smiles. It was like he practiced them in front of mirrors. I had almost forgotten how much Larry liked to kid around. Then I remembered how all last summer he pretended to be different people. One time he even pretended to be a storm trooper with a crazy German accent.

My mother made all kinds of apologies for not being able to offer him anything. "We've barely un-packed yet," she said. The second anyone sets foot in our house my mother always starts bringing out the food.

"How's your omelettes, Gordie?" he asked, drop-ping the accent. "I can still taste the sour-cream-and-prune one." He pretended to double over with pain and throw up. We all laughed. I even heard Myra break up.

"It stopped raining," said my mother, who was struggling to open a window. Larry went to help her and opened it without too much trouble. That's something else about Larry—he can come in and sort of take over.

My mother thanked him and said, "You must be a real help around the house."

I felt kind of finky, because I knew if I was at Larry's and his mother's window got stuck, it would remain stuck. I'm not so big on taking over and I'm also rotten at fixing things. A few times I even broke pickle jars just getting the lids off.

Larry recovered his accent and said, "Hey, Pardner, can you split from the ranch for a while?"

"Yes, he can split from the ranch if he goes to get me shelving paper," said my mother, who was back on her shelving-paper routine.

Larry said he'd walk me to the store. When we got outside, the first thing he talked about was how wild he thought it was, me getting stuck in crazy Kravitz's bungalow. "When I heard about it I laughed myself sick," he said, trying to force another good laugh. I pretended that the whole thing was a big joke and I smiled an idiot kind of smile.

"We sure nearly scared her to death," he said, grabbing the back of my neck and squeezing too tight. I threw my head back, and he took his hand off and stopped laughing. Then he said, "Boy, Myra's getting big boobs."

That was something I really didn't want to hear.

I mean like it's all right to talk about someone else, but it seemed kind of dumb to hear talk like that about my own sister.

"Did you get any this winter?" Larry teased, and tried to tickle my sides. I knew he was dying for me to ask him about his sex life and I really wanted to, but I just kept cool and didn't say anything. Anyway, I knew it wouldn't take too long before he'd volunteer all kinds of details about his sexual conquests.

"Hey, man, did I have a winter, wow!" He shook his hand as if he'd just touched something hot.

Then Larry began to play my game and he didn't say anything else. And I just clammed up.

Although it stopped raining, the sun still didn't come out, and everything was gray and soggy-looking. A lot of the younger kids were playing tag along the paths, and Dee Dee Levenson ran up to us and asked if I was going to put on a puppet show like I did last year.

I once saw these puppets on TV, and I sort of got turned on to them. I mean if you look at puppets long enough they almost seem kind of real and crazy in a good way.

Well anyway, I went to the library and took out all these books on puppets. The first one I made was so-so, but then I made another one and it really turned out pretty good, and I learned how to work it also. So then I made a few more.

I even made one that looked like Lucille Ball—everybody said it looked like her. Some people said that if I sent her a photo of it she'd probably have me on her TV show with it. That seemed like a dumb idea and I never did it.

But I did put on a sort of TV comedy for the bungalow kids last year, and they really ate it up. I got a big charge out of it also. At the time, Larry said, "*Jeez*, is that all you can play with?"

I was sorry, in a way, Dee Dee said anything about the puppets. Larry looked at me strangely, and said with a German accent, "I hope you aren't playing vis dolls anymore—you know vat ve say about little boys who play mit dolls."

I wanted to say, "I'm not a little boy and they're not dolls." Instead I said, "I haven't touched them since last summer." But I was lying.

Dee Dee walked with us and held on to my hand. But she let go screaming when Avram Hurwitz tagged her from behind. He chased her along the narrow path, and then they both disappeared behind one of the bungalows.

The wet sand soaked through my sneakers, making a light slapping sound when I walked. I looked down at them and then at Larry's. I was really curious about Larry's painted sneakers.

"Where did you get those crazy sneakers?" I asked.

Larry raised one foot in front of him. "You like 'em? I painted them myself."

"Yeah, they're all right," I said. "Why the Stars of David, and what do the other designs mean?"

Larry looked at me and contorted his face into a strange expression. "They're secret symbols," he said.

"What's so secret about a Jewish star?" I said. Larry looked at me with a boy-are-you-dumb look on his face.

"That's no ordinary Jewish star," he said. "It's also a symbol from black magic."

"Black magic?" I said. "What do you know about black magic?"

I can be real cool about a lot of things, but Larry was playing a good game, and suddenly it was really important that I know about his sneakers.

But Larry just smiled. I'd seen his smile on teachers' faces before they flunked you.

"Okay," I said to myself, "so Larry has another routine."

On the porch of our old bungalow, where the wheelchair had been, there was now the biggest doll-house in existence. I mean I had just never seen one like it. And in it tons of furniture. It was just fantastic. It had little rugs and lamps, and even the bathroom had a roll of tiny toilet paper. It reminded me of something I'd read about in *Ripley's Believe It or Not*. There was some thirteenth-century monk who carved furniture that fit on the heads of pins. Things like that really ruin me.

"It's for a family of midgets," said Larry. For some reason I didn't want to say anything about the wheelchair I'd seen there before, but Larry told me about it. And he asked me if I knew who it belonged to.

Irwin Friedman ran by wearing his Blue Channel lifeguard shirt. He said, "Hello," and then pretended to dive into an imaginary wave. He shouted, "Watch out for the big ones."

"Who'll save *you*?" Larry yelled out after him.

When we got to Siegel's Cut-Rate Variety Store and Mr. Siegel saw Larry, he said, "Not you again."

There was a whole thing last summer where he accused Larry of stealing some model-making glue. Larry's mother really got on to him about how her boy wouldn't do a thing like that, and even my mother said, "How can he accuse a nice polite boy like Larry of stealing?" Anyway, he didn't have any proof and the whole thing blew over.

I didn't think too much of Mr. Siegel, who all summer long wore the same crummy pink-and-green-flowered shirt. And he also wore a dumb straw hat with a scroungy feather stuck in it. This year the shirt was different but just as rotten-looking, and the hat was the same. I'm sure the feather came off of some diseased bird. His store was a mess like he was, and he had to look through heaps of garbage before he found the shelving paper.

When we got out of the store, Larry had a crap-eating expression on. "Hey Gordie, do you want your sneakers to look like mine?"

I just looked at him without saying anything. I mean I just hadn't thought about it, and decisions like that take a little thinking over. So I looked down at Larry's sneakers and studied them for a while, and the only thing I could come up with was, "I don't know."

"Come on!" he said taking out about a half dozen Magic Markers from his pocket. "Don't you want to belong to the League of Demons?"

"Where did you get those Magic Markers from?" I asked, real dumb, as if I didn't know. I just hoped

Mr. Siegel wasn't planning on taking inventory too soon.

Larry made a quick red stroke on one of my sneakers. "Now you have to let me do it," he said.

I'm real easy sometimes, and anyway I figured there's no harm in it, so I went ahead and let Larry have a go at my sneakers.

We sat on the bench outside the laundromat while Larry really had a ball with the Magic Markers. He went at it with a terrific amount of enthusiasm. All the while he's telling me about things like the cults of Satan and how black magic means power.

When he was all finished, he looked at my sneakers as if he had just painted the Mona Lisa. "Now you're one of us," he grinned. "And what really makes your sneakers so special is that they were done with stolen Magic Markers, and of course the fact that I'm left-handed also helps matters."

"Boy, aren't I lucky," I wisecracked, looking down at my sneakers. Some of the colors had run into each other because my sneakers were wet, and I could barely make out the Stars of David, which really looked like runny triangles.

Then I got a crazy feeling for about a minute. I was afraid to walk in my sneakers, like I almost expected something to happen.

When I left Larry, he shouted after me, "Going to the boardwalk tonight?"

"I don't know," I hollered back without even turning. Some of the colors from my sneakers were beginning to come through onto my feet, and the whole thing seemed like a great big mistake. I put the roll of shelving paper up to my lips to howl through it, then I lost the urge. Instead I put it up to my eye like a telescope and I focused on our porch. I saw Myra talking to Irwin.

4

GYPSY GRANDMA

It was a real foggy night, and you could hear Lonesome Pete wailing from one end of the boardwalk to the other. Lonesome Pete was the name I'd given to an old cowboy singer who sang at the Texas Bar.

There weren't too many people out, and a lot of the places still hadn't opened up for the season. Even Luna Land, the amusement park, was still closed. I had heard some talk about it being torn down for a housing development, but it must have been a rumor because there were signs all around announcing its opening in a few days.

The lights along the boardwalk looked blurry, like when you cry. I headed in the direction of the Texas Bar, which opened out onto the boardwalk.

During the summer a lot of the kids hung around in front of it at night. The bar was owned by a big red-headed lady named Dolores Monahan who was also bartender. From time to time she'd chase the kids away, saying, "This ain't no hangout for kids," or "Beat it before the cops get on my tail." She talked like a hood's moll from an old movie. I used to get some dumb charge out of hearing her talk. Sometimes I'd go in the place and pretend I had to go to the bathroom just to hear her say something like, "Take your piss someplace else, this ain't no public john."

Inside the bar, it was all blue mirrors and pictures of Dolores Monahan when she was young and in some kind of show business. One time when I looked at the pictures and I looked at her behind the bar I got an awful feeling. I mean like I felt sorry for her that she had to get older. I got that feeling once when I looked at my parents' wedding picture, like it's really funny and in a way almost scary how people change.

There was a new Lonesome Pete sitting on top of the round bar. He was different from the other one—this new guy was young and real good-looking, like some guy you'd expect to see in a TV series. He had a white-and-silver guitar, and he didn't sing

28

half bad. The more I looked at him, the more out of place he seemed at the Texas Bar. There were only two people in the place, and suddenly I felt sorry for the guy. I can feel sorry for people real easy when they don't seem to be making out too great. Sometimes I give money to beggars, because if I think real hard about them not eating, or sleeping out in the streets, I begin to feel rotten. It's a whole mixed-up feeling of me having it and them not, and then what if someday I shouldn't have it and I'd hope someone would give me a handout.

I stood in front of the bar and there weren't any other kids there. I knew Larry was going to show, but it was the kind of night that makes you feel really alone. I was almost sorry I went out. Earlier I had asked Myra if she wanted to play cards, but she said she had things to do. And my father had arrived with the other suitcases and he fell dead asleep. My mother told me to stay in, but I told her I didn't feel like spending the whole night watching her put on shelving paper.

"I say there, Dr. Watson, foggy night, isn't it?" Larry came up from behind me and spoke in an English accent.

"To be sure," I answered in my best English accent.

"It's a night for crime," Larry chuckled.

"I say, Mr. Holmes, you'd best watch out for Professor Moriarty on a night such as this!" My English accent was getting good.

But then Larry turned it all off and extended his lower teeth over his top lip and made some really crazy horror face and said, "I am the evil Professor Moriarty!" He made his voice quiver. Then he pretended to choke me.

"Okay, cut the crap!" I said trying to come off real bored, but in a way I was bothered.

"Don't scoff at a son of Satan," he said in an almost serious way. "You only have to look at your sneakers to remember you're one of us!"

"Look at my sneakers," I said. "They look ruined to me, and when I took them off even my feet had that stupid color all over them."

"Black magic at work," he said very casually. "By now the colors should be in your bloodstream."

I began to think about the colors from the Magic Markers entering my bloodstream and my blood turning rainbow color.

Wanting to change the subject, I said, "Most everything's still closed."

"Amusement-O-Rama is open," said Larry, getting more normal.

"I don't have too much money," I said.

"That's okay, I do," said Larry.

Larry's mother and father were divorced and Larry was the only child, and every time his father came around he loaded Larry down with money. Larry's father must have been pretty rich, because one time when I asked my father for extra money, he said, "What do you think—I'm a wealthy man like Larry's father?"

Larry sometimes treated, but most of the time I paid him back. Amusement-O-Rama was a big garage kind of building, and it was filled with pinball machines and a skeetball game. There was also the big roulette wheel, Fortune's Turn. You could win anything from a key ring to a big stuffed animal. Which for some reason Myra was dying to get last summer. Most girls really go nuts over stuffed toys.

Coming in from the dark, the bright lights inside just about knocked me out. Gypsy Grandma, the wax fortune teller with the stuffed owl on her shoulder, sat in a glass booth in the entranceway. For a cent she'd move her head and hand over a deck of cards, and then a fortune would fall from a slot. In a way she was kind of eerie with her lifelike glass eyes that seemed to recognize people. If I ever told

31

anyone about it they'd think I was nuts, but at times I thought she really knew me.

One time I got a fortune from her and it said, "Someone close will soon cause trouble." A few weeks after that Myra threatened to rat on me when she caught me smoking.

I couldn't pass up Gypsy Grandma. I mean it would be like not saying hello to an old friend. So I blew a cent. Old Grandma was beginning to look kind of seedy. Part of her face had melted a little, and her pet owl had begun to molt. She also seemed to move slower this year.

"Okay, what does it say?" said Larry, practically on top of me. I tried to read it very mysteriously.

"Someone out of the past will come back into your life."

"V-e-e-e-e-ry interesting!" said Larry, who threw a penny in.

Old Grandma lifted her hand and got frozen into position. "I think she's run out of messages," I said.

Larry stuck up his middle finger. "Screw you too, Grandma!" he shouted.

Some tough-looking girls who I figured must have come over from the Bath Beach section, a real tough neighborhood, were hanging around the jukebox listening to some group moaning, "Ah Wha, Whaaa, Whaaa, Whaaa, Whaaa!"

Larry said they were quick pieces. "We could have any one of them under the boardwalk," he said.

"They look real tough to me," I said. And I was sorry the second after I said it because I knew what was going to come from Larry.

"What are you, some kind of fruit pie?" he said, in a real put-down kind of voice.

But the funny thing is Larry didn't go near them. Not only that, but it seemed to me he purposely avoided them by going down a different aisle. But he still kept up the dumb tease; I mean he just wouldn't drop it. "What's the matter, Wolfman doesn't want any action?"

I felt like telling Larry to cut the crap about his being a big make-out artist and just leaving him there, but for some reason I can't do things like that, so I kept my mouth shut and hung around.

Larry began to play the pinball machines and I walked over to Fortune's Turn. The whole idea was to put a dime down on a big board with lots of names on it, and if the roulette wheel stopped on the name you chose you got to win something. To get the big stuffed animal you had to win two in a row. I think only once I saw someone win an animal. I watched a few people play awhile, and then I put a dime down on the name Fritzi, a name I liked from the comic strip "Nancy." The guy turned the wheel and I nearly croaked when it landed on Fritzi. Like all last summer I played and never won anything. "Give that gentleman a prize!" said the guy who ran the game. His helper was a beat-up looking blonde lady who looked like one big sweat stain. She handed me a goldfish in a bowl and smiled. Her few remaining teeth looked like they were covered with mossy slime. I gave her a big smile back and took my prize.

I tried to hide a little of my excitement when I went over to Larry with the goldfish. "Hey, look what I won!" I said.

"Big deal, a ten-cent goldfish!" he said. It *was* a big deal in a way. Sure, anyone can go out and buy one, but it's really different when you win one. It makes it all special. I didn't want to explain anything like that to Larry because I'm sure he knew it. I figured he was a little envious.

"I'm going to call it Fritzi," I said.

"Fritzi Titzie," laughed Larry. He laughed hard at his own joke. I stood around and watched Larry play another few games of pinball, and when the board lit up TILT, Larry yelled, "It's fixed!" He yelled loud enough for the tough-looking girls at the jukebox to hear, because they all looked at us. I pretended not to see them—they sort of gave me the creeps.

We left the place and walked along the board-walk. It was very quiet and you could hear the waves breaking. "Let's see Fritzi," said Larry. I held the fishbowl up, and Larry grabbed it out of my hands. "Let's make a sacrifice to Satan," he said.

"What do you mean, sacrifice?" I said, trying to grab it back, but Larry held the bowl tight.

"That's part of being a follower of Satan," he said. "You've got to sacrifice living things."

"Well, I'm no follower of Satan!" I said. "And all that black magic stuff, I don't even know what it means."

"Gordie boy, the moment you let me paint your sneakers, you were a member of the cult."

"Oh baloney!" I said, getting kind of mad. "I mean, that might be the dumbest thing I've heard."

"Black magic might surprise you," said Larry. "I've been collecting a few spells."

"Okay, Mr. Spell Collector, can I just have my goldfish back?" I said, once again trying to grab it.

Larry spilled a little water out of the bowl. "Why don't we sacrifice it slowly?"

I didn't know whether to play Larry's game or

just say, "Screw you, Larry Perl." I didn't know if Larry was kidding or not, and I got the feeling he didn't either. Then I walked ahead of Larry and he put his arm around my shoulder and gave me back the goldfish.

We walked without saying anything, and when we came to the Breeze Front Hotel, Larry said, "Come on, let's see what's happening here."

When I said, "It's late. I'd better go home," Larry said, "Boy, you're really turning into a drag. I'm not too sure I shouldn't have listened to my mother and gone to the country this summer."

I suddenly felt as if I was ruining Larry's good time. He had a talent for making me feel that.

The Breeze Front bordered on the boardwalk, and we sneaked onto one of the porches. A lot of the rooms were still empty, with mattresses rolled up on the beds. The Breeze Front was really kind of marked down; it was like a big fire trap. During the summer you saw mostly old people there, or if there was a family you could bet they weren't too well-off.

"Last year I found a whole box of contraceptives in one of the rooms," said Larry. Then he went on to brag. "I sure made use of them during the year."

"What did you use them for, balloons at a party?" I said, laughing at my own joke.

"Very funny, big man. I know more about things like that than you'll ever know." Larry began to jump up and down on one of the beds like it was a trampoline. I put down the goldfish and joined in. As we jumped up and down we began to pull the light string over the bed. I pulled too hard and broke the string, turning the light off and leaving the room in complete darkness.

Then I heard a lady hollering on the porch below, "What's going on up there? I'm going to call the police." Larry got away fast, but my foot got stuck in a bedspring. My getaway seemed to take forever, and when I finally freed myself I ran out of the room leaving my goldfish behind. I knew there was no going back for it, and I really felt rotten. Larry was nowhere in sight.

Most of the lights were out in the bungalows, and only the porch light was on at ours. I sat on the front steps for a while and tried to get my breath. I'd run all the way. I looked down the row of bungalows, and in our old one I could see the blue flickering light of a TV. It was real quiet, and then I thought I heard my name being called. It was a voice I didn't know. It almost sounded like an old lady, as if Gypsy Grandma could really speak. I ran into the bungalow and got into bed, covering my head with the blanket.

5

BAD DREAMS

I was really happy to see some morning light come
into the bungalow. I mean at Steiners' you can't
expect a sunburst, but it was good to see shadowy
humps become things like chairs and tables. All
night long I'd had rotten kinds of dreams that kept
waking me up and getting me scared and making
me feel all alone. I don't mind being alone, but being
scared and alone is different.

One dream just about sent my heart popping out
of my chest. I dreamed that I was all alone in the
bungalow, and I knew I was alone, because for some
reason I had checked all the rooms. And then after
I made a check of the whole place, I walked out onto
the porch. I stood on the porch awhile looking out,

then I heard the front door slam behind me. I looked around and saw this lady all in black, with a black hat too, and like I knew she was some evil kind of thing. Boy, did it shake me up. I suppose because I dreamed about the bungalow and not some far-out place, it all seemed more real in a way, and those are always the worst kind of dreams.

My feet were out from under the covers and I could still see some of the color on them from Larry's handiwork. I looked at my feet for a long time, and the more I looked at them, the more it seemed as if they were two things that didn't belong to me, like they were really no part of me. I moved my toes but that didn't help change my feeling.

It was like I was seeing them for the first time. Sometimes you see something a lot, and you think you know that thing pretty well, and then it happens for one quick second that you really see it. I mean it's like really seeing it for the first time, and you know what it's all about. I guess it can happen with almost anything, a chair, or a person. And afterward —well, sometimes that thing goes right on being what it always was, and sometimes it's never the same again.

A fly buzzed on the flypaper that hung from the light above the kitchen table. "Dopey fly," I whispered. He really put up a terrific fight to get off of it. I almost felt like freeing him, but I knew his wings would still be stuck to the paper, and a fly without wings is out of business anyway. His buzzing seemed real loud, and I'm sure in fly language he was yelling for help.

I thought about Larry's sacrifice-for-Satan routine, and the goldfish and about what a Pinocchio I'd been. That's what I call myself when I do dumb jerky things like not listening to myself and listening to someone like a Larry Perl instead. And the funny thing is that I know beforehand I'm going to get messed up in some way, but I go along all the same. I wondered if I should go back to the Breeze Front and try to find the goldfish, but I'm really too chicken to run the risk of getting caught. I could almost imagine that hollering lady just lying in wait for me. I tried to make myself feel better by picturing the old screaming lady taking care of the goldfish and really loving it, and it becoming the most important thing in her life. And in a way I won a prize for her.

But I was feeding myself a lot of baloney, because the more I thought about it, the more it bothered me about losing that fish. I practically got an ache thinking about it. And there wasn't anyone I could tell it to. If I did tell someone, it would almost be the same as putting a commercial on TV telling everyone that you're a dumb jerk.

I heard a noise on the front porch, and all the thoughts in my head disappeared like down a drain. I listened hard. It was the rocking chair. At first I was too scared to investigate. Then I looked from behind the window curtain. I saw my mother. I figured she must have been out there a long time. She looked like she was into some deep thoughts. It wasn't like my mother to just get up and sit on the porch. When my mother gets up, it's when breakfast begins and the household chores get started. The more I looked at her, the more she seemed to be very alone. I put my pants on and went onto the porch.

I must have startled her when I came out, because she let out a little cry and she blinked and opened her eyes wide. Then she sighed, the kind of sigh that always came before some illness-type complaint like, "Do I have a headache!" or "Does my neck hurt!"

"What a dream I had!" she said.

I felt like saying, "Me too!" but I didn't. I kept it to myself.

My mother looked tired, and without her glasses on I could really look into her eyes and I could see unhappiness.

"Come, Gordie, let's go inside." My mother got out of the rocker like it was some big effort.

Inside, she began to talk loud enough for Myra and my father to hear her, so even if they had been asleep her talking would have gotten them up for sure.

"All night long I dreamed about Widow Kravitz. She looked terrible, and she was trying to grab onto you and Myra."

Storybook pictures of Hansel and Gretel came to me. Only it was like Myra and I were Hansel and Gretel, and I imagined Widow Kravitz as the old witch.

There's one thing about my mother that's kind of scary. I mean aside from her feelings about things that are going to happen, it's her dreams that are really spooky.

I remember a time one morning she woke up and told us about this dream she had about a man she once worked for who died a long time ago. Well, she dreamed that this dead guy's wife was about to go into business with some other guy, and he told my mother to tell her not to do it.

All that day my mother talked about that dream, until she said, "I know you'll all think I'm crazy, but I'm going to call Mrs. Waxman." (That was her ex-boss's name, Waxman.)

My father told her she was crazy. Crazy or not, my mother went through the phone book and called her up. Then my mother told her the dream. You could have knocked us over when this Mrs. Waxman told my mother that she was planning on getting a business partner. A few days later she called my mother back and told her that my mother's call made her decide not to go into business with the guy.

Now I got to admit that's kind of weird. My father says it was a coincidence. But between her feelings and her dreams, my mother has a pretty good batting average.

My father got out of bed and joined my mother and me at the breakfast table.

Myra came into the room wearing Widow Kravitz's hat. "Will you please leave my bungalow," she said, faking an old lady's voice with a Yiddish accent.

We all laughed except my mother, who looked scared at first, and then she got angry and pulled the hat off of Myra's head.

"You asking for trouble?" my mother yelled. "You don't fool around with things like that."

"I was only kidding," said Myra.

"More trouble comes from kidding than you think," said my mother.

6

THE CHANGES

Breakfast was finished in silence. My bran flakes tasted like sawdust. My father left for work. And Myra left for her steady baby-sitting job. She was helping out Mrs. Hurwitz, who had a new baby. Myra thought babies were the absolute end. When she left I told her to "have a good time with the diapers and all the stuff in them."

She said she couldn't wait until she was married and had a baby of her own.

When she told me that, I told her if she repeated it, I'd vomit! Then she went into a thing about how disgusting I can get. I can't help it if I'm not so crazy about babies.

I sat on the porch and I knew it was going to be

a good beach day, but I really wasn't in the mood for it. I wasn't much in the mood for anything. My mother scrubbed the floors and then made a newspaper path from the front door to the bathroom.

She said, "Why don't you put on your new bathing suit?"

"New bathing suit?" It really broke me up. My new bathing suit was one of my cousin Myron's cast-offs and it was about as new as a covered wagon. Not only was it old, but it was also the ugliest maroon color and it had repairs in some embarrassing places.

When I wanted to go back into the bungalow, the picture of a bloody-faced woman whose husband had just been killed in an auto accident looked up at me. It just didn't seem decent to step on her face, so I jumped over her and messed the newspapers up.

My mother really let go with some hollering. For as long as I could remember my mother hollered a lot, but I noticed that in the past few weeks she seemed really nervous and hollered more. When I once talked to Myra about it, she said it came from woman troubles, and that my mother was going through her changes.

I didn't know what she meant by that, and when

I pressed her, she just said, "You're too immature, you wouldn't understand."

I dropped it, but it bothered me. It seemed like the bungalow didn't help my mother much, because this hat thing really had her going now.

My mother looked at the hat as if it held the key to some great mystery. "I'm going to have to ask Mr. Steiner where Widow Kravitz lives." She looked at the hat some more and whispered, "If she's still living."

Then I said something that I hoped would discourage my mother from doing anything more about the hat except forgetting it. I told her that I heard that Mr. Steiner was spending the whole summer on a remote island in the Thousand Islands and that he couldn't be reached. And I told her the reason he was doing that was because all last summer the bungalow people bothered him at all hours for every little thing—like a dripping faucet or a broken window.

"That's funny," said my mother. "I had heard that Mr. Steiner was spending the summer with his married son in California."

"It isn't so," I said. "That's what he wants everyone to believe."

I suddenly felt very sorry about making up the whole dumb story.

Dropping the hat into a shopping bag, my mother said, "Don't ever touch this!" Then she put it away in the closet.

I wondered what would happen if I just threw the stupid thing away, and I couldn't understand why my mother didn't.

"Why don't we throw it away?" I said. "It's already in the bag."

"Because it's a good hat! And until I find out why she left it here, here it will stay! Besides, who knows, one of these days she might turn up at the door asking for it."

The thought of Widow Kravitz at the front door made me feel uncomfortable.

I put the bathing suit on and wrapped a towel around it. Then I went out again and sat on the porch railing, facing in.

I thought about my mother's awful dream, and I wished I hadn't heard about it, especially after the one I had. It was like there was a shadow over the bungalow, and it seemed as if we should just pack our bags and leave.

With all the gloomy predictions, something had

to happen for sure. It made me think of times I might have been doing something all right, and then someone comes along and tells me to be careful, and that's when it usually happens the whole thing gets messed up. I just think certain things shouldn't be brought to anyone's attention.

All at once I felt myself losing my balance as I was grabbed from behind.

"Okay, officer, I have him! This is the midnight menace, otherwise known as the Wolfman!"

"Cut the crap, Larry," I said, holding on tightly to the railing.

"I'll bet we really shook up that old lady at the Breeze Front last night!" He said it like it was some big accomplishment.

"Yeah, it was a riot," I said. And from the tone of my voice, Larry knew what I really meant.

"How is the prize goldfish?" he asked.

I told him what had happened. He said he was sorry, and I could tell he meant it.

"I suppose it's my fault," he said.

I couldn't blame Larry for losing the fish. I always hated kids who blamed someone else when something happened to them. I was kind of annoyed at myself. It would have been stupid to blame Larry.

Larry was wearing a new yellow bathing suit, and his towel was around his neck. "Come on, I'll race you to the beach!" he said.

It was like someone pressed a button in me, and I automatically started running.

"Last one there is a fag!" he shouted. He had a big head start, but it didn't take long for me to pass him up, and when I did that he stopped running and said, "No fair, my sneakers are untied."

"Bull crap!" I shouted when I got to the beach, and I gave out with a wolfcall.

I threw off my towel and ran into the water. It was cold and dirty. Larry came in splashing after me. We started kidding around until the lifeguard blew his whistle.

We got out of the water and walked along the rock jetty searching for crabs. The designs on Larry's sneakers were disappearing fast.

"Well, there goes another follower of Satan," I said, pointing to his sneakers.

"Oh, that doesn't matter. It's what's here and here that matters!" he said, pointing to his head and heart.

I didn't know if Larry's Satan thing was something he really believed, half believed or pretended.

So when I asked him if he believed in curses from people dead or alive, he answered, "Yes!" right away.

He went into this thing about how we receive radio and television messages through airwaves and how people's thoughts can be transmitted through airwaves also. And how when people die their thoughts, good and bad, can be left hanging around in places.

I pictured opening all the windows and the door in the bungalow and having a great wind sweep through the place, getting rid of anything that might have been left there. What Larry said to me seemed to make sense in some crazy kind of way.

That's one thing I had to say about Larry. He knew about a lot of different things. He wasn't a real brain, it was just that he knew about certain things that other kids didn't.

We sat on the rocks and collected seaweed with our feet. We watched our feet and legs gradually disappear under a load of the stuff.

I wondered if Larry had ever heard anything about the change of life women go through. Not wanting to come out with just another question, I said, very matter of factly, "Do you know that women go through changes of life?"

"Sure!" he said. "And sometimes it sends them to the nut house."

I imagined my mother being carted off in a straitjacket wearing Widow Kravitz's hat.

"It's called menopause," he said, popping the seaweed around his feet.

Menopause—it sounded like the name of some ancient ruler from the lost continent of Atlantis.

"I guess it must be tough on women when they realize that they can't have any more kids. They don't get their period anymore and it's something they've been used to for a long time and I suppose when they lose it, it must shake them up. Probably some more than others. It's just a whole big change that takes place." Larry finished talking and threw a ball of seaweed back into the water.

I figured Larry had to know what he was talking about. Because even Myra couldn't wait until she had babies, and I suppose when she got older and she found out she couldn't have them anymore it would probably upset her a lot.

I was suddenly feeling sorry for my mother and Myra, and wishing they didn't have to go through it.

"Gordie, it's much easier being a man." Larry stretched out on the rocks.

51

"You said it."

Different pictures of my mother going crazy came into my head. I imagined my mother putting up a fierce struggle as some big guard tossed her into a padded cell.

I had a tremendous urge to run home.

7

JOB AVAILABLE

All the way back to the bungalow, I wondered if my mother was going crazy and if it had started already. I still wasn't too sure about this whole menopause thing, but it sounded terrible. A lot of times it's best not knowing about something, and what is even worse is knowing half of something.

When I got back to the bungalow my mother was on the porch, sewing and listening to the radio. She didn't look up when I got there—she was deep into the radio program. From what I could make out it was some women's program and they were discussing sex before marriage. When some woman said she thought it was important for a couple to live together for a while before marriage, I heard my mother say, "Sounds like a prostitute talking."

For the first time she looked up at me and said, "Nice girls get married first. This whole sexual freedom thing today is going to lead to another Sodom and Gomorrah."

I looked at my mother and wondered if what she said made sense. While I was in the bungalow changing, I heard my mother calling me. When I finished I went on the porch.

She turned off the radio, put down her sewing and took off her glasses.

I tried hard to look into her eyes. I had heard somewhere that you could always tell if someone was crazy by the look in their eyes. It was hard for me to tell—my mother was squinting.

"Irwin was here looking for you," she said. "It almost slipped my mind, and it's important."

"What did he want?"

"He said they need a junior counselor at the day camp."

"Did you tell him I wasn't looking for a job?"

"No," said my mother, putting her glasses back on and looking at me in a strange way. "He remembered how last summer you put on the puppet show, and how much the children liked it, and you. He thought you'd be qualified for the job."

"But that was different—it was because I wanted to do it!"

"The only difference is you'll be getting paid for the work."

I knew my mother couldn't understand that things are different when you do them yourself and when someone wants you to do it. I suddenly saw the entire summer pass before me with me a prisoner in a day camp.

"Anyway, I don't know anything about being a counselor."

"What's to know?" said my mother. "You'll learn."

"Well, I don't want it!" I shouted.

The second after I shouted, I was sorry, because I could see my mother beginning to get nervous.

I just wanted to get away before a whole scene erupted. I could just see my mother going berserk.

Then she went right on talking as if she hadn't heard one word I said.

"He said that you should report for the interview tomorrow morning. We're in luck too," she said. "I packed a nice dress shirt, tie and slacks for you, in case of an emergency."

My mother and I had different ideas about what

emergencies were. And suddenly she's saying, "We're in luck," like she's going for the job too.

I walked along the narrow paths around the bungalows, and wherever I saw seashell boundaries and designs I either crunched them or kicked sand over them, hiding them.

The whole idea of camp life seemed like a lot of crap. That's why I hated school so much—you're always being told what to do. And as if that wasn't bad enough, there was the bull crap I went through when I hit a high pop fly right into the hands of the pitcher, or listened to remarks like, "What do you have, a hole in your hand, Gordie?" when I missed the ball playing the outfield.

I was happy to be away from all that. And the good thing about summer was doing what I wanted to do. The whole job thing scared me.

When I got back to the bungalow Myra was there. I couldn't have been there more than three seconds when she started on me.

"Gordie, I think it's terrific about the possibility of your being a junior counselor."

I never thought Myra would turn out to be a traitor. I mean we argued, but I never thought she'd turn against me.

I suddenly looked at Myra and got kind of mad

and yelled, "So how come *you* don't become a counselor?"

"Because I have a steady job baby-sitting this summer."

"But that's not a *job* job!" I shouted.

Then my mother piped in with something that really made me wonder about her. She said, "She's a girl and you're a boy."

I wanted to shout, "You have just won a year's supply of elephant dung for that deduction," but I kept my mouth shut because I knew my mother's hysterical voice would come onto the scene like an earthquake.

My mother started again, and I felt as if I was being bombarded from all directions. They didn't know what it was like to be ripped apart for being a lousy athlete. I mean it was all right for Irwin— he was always dribbling a basketball or swinging a bat. But I hated being rotten at something and having the whole world see it. Anyway, I just wanted to be left alone.

Myra tried to calm the whole thing down by saying, "First of all, they're not handing you the job. You have to be interviewed."

Even the idea of a job interview shook me up. "Interview" was such a stiff word, something that belonged with school, and it had no place being used in the summer.

"That's right," said my mother. "They're not giving such good jobs away so easily."

I knew my mother's game. It was like I was a real kid again, and if I didn't eat she threatened to give my food to a good child who deserved it. It used to work, but it didn't make the food taste any better.

"What's a summer for if not to have a good time?" I couldn't hide the quiver in my voice. Like I really wanted to cry. It was almost like a final plea.

"My God!" said Myra. "You'd think you were going off to war. The job is only five days a week— you'll have off Saturday and Sunday if you get it!" Then she looked me straight in the eyes. I turned my head because I didn't want her to see how I felt. "Anyway," she continued, "I think the whole idea is ridiculous. With your attitude you're just not mature enough to be a junior counselor."

That night when my father came home, he sided with them. He looked so tired and miserable from his job that I thought for sure he'd side with me and say, "Gordie, there's plenty of time for work." But he didn't. He said, "It sounds like a good chance to make a little money."

When everyone was in bed I sat on the porch and

looked up at the sky, and there was almost a full moon. I really wished I had the power to turn into a werewolf. Then no one would mess around with me for sure.

"Gordie, go to bed," my mother called. "You have to be there early tomorrow."

I went into the bungalow and lay in bed with my arms behind my head. I thought about Widow Kravitz's thoughts clinging to the walls. And I whispered, "Get out of here, you're not wanted."

Sometimes I think I'm going to go crazy.

8

THE INTERVIEW

I walked along the boardwalk and thought about the speech my mother had given me, one that she had told me to tell the man in charge of the day camp. I had his name written on a scrap of paper and it was slowly disintegrating from me looking at it so much. I couldn't remember if his name was Morgan Stanley or Stanley Morgan. Just my luck I had to have an interview with a guy that had two first names.

"How do you do, Mr. Morgan? Mr. Stanley? I'm Gordon Cassman."

"Remember," my mother had said, "your name is Gordon, not Gordie. Gordie is for children and you are a young man applying for a job."

I said to my mother, "So how come you always call me Gordie?"

And she says, "To me, you'll always be my little Gordie."

It's hard to win with my mother. "Mr. Morgan? Mr. Stanley? I think I am highly qualified for the position of junior counselor because my mother told me to tell you that, but it's all really a lot of crap. Because truthfully, I'm scared about the whole thing. I mean I've worked before. I delivered orders for Tabor's Market, but that was different because I've known Mr. and Mrs. Tabor all my life, and because I see all the kids I know when I make deliveries. Anyway, my mother is going crazy and she sent me here."

The sun was really out in full force, and I could tell it was going to be a terrific beach day. Blue Channel Day Camp was all the way at one end of the boardwalk. Luna Land was at the other end. The glass dome of Luna Land really sparkled in the morning sunshine. It almost looked like some space station sending out messages.

People were beginning to run across the boardwalk in bathing suits, and I felt like a real outcast with my shirt and strangling tie on.

"How do you do? I'm Gordon Cassman and I

know nothing about being a junior counselor, so you see, Mr. Morgan? Mr. Stanley? this whole thing is one big mistake, sorry!"

I mean the "How do you do?" line is such a phony thing, I don't even think I could get past that part of my mother's speech. I never say "How do you do?" to anyone. It just sounds silly, like something out of an old movie. I always say "Hello" when I meet someone. My mother has her own set of rules, like it's proper to do this and that at such a particular time. That's okay for my mother but it doesn't work for me. And the whole tie idea seemed so stupid. I was really beginning to sweat around my neck. Boy, do I hate meeting new people. I think I'd rather stay locked up in my room sometimes than meet new people. And what's really awful is when you have to meet new people and they judge you. Another one of the reasons I hate school so much is the time when I get new teachers. Boy, is that an ordeal! I'm really lousy when it comes to making a good first impression.

This girl I know at school, Phyllis Lavine, once told me that when she first saw me she didn't like me, and it wasn't until a long while after she knew me that she liked me. I thought about it a lot. And when I asked her why she didn't like me at first, she said it was hard to explain, but I seemed kind of different—just a loner.

Passing Dolores Monahan's Texas Bar, I could smell the disinfectant that had just been used to mop the tile floors. The blue mirrors on the walls were reflected in the wet and shiny floors, and it almost looked like water and sky.

Dolores Monahan was behind the bar cleaning up from the night before. Even though it was early morning, she had a customer. I recognized him— he was the janitor from the Sea Breeze. He was a real oddball and kind of strange-looking. I wondered if he looked that way because of the way he acted, or if he acted that way because of the way he looked. It seemed like his chin was being swallowed up into his neck, and when he looked up from his glass he was like a real turtlehead. I remembered last summer when he got real drunk, he'd yell things, and his favorite expression was, "In your mother's hat!"

It really used to break me up, because I'd imagine doing all sorts of things in one of my mother's hats.

I stopped walking and looked out toward the ocean. There was a kind of haze over it. My thoughts went to Widow Kravitz's hat and how I wished my mother had never found it. For some dumb reason it seemed like it was screwing everything up.

The shirt I was wearing began to stick to me. The sun was really beating down, and I was beginning to get uncomfortable. I began to plot how I'd tell my mother they didn't want me for the job because they thought I looked like such a creep in the tie and shirt. I began to do some serious thinking about not showing up for the interview. The only problem in that was it would get back to my mother through Irwin.

I thought about Larry, and wondered who he'd pal around with if I got the job.

As I got nearer to the end of the boardwalk and closer to the camp, I got a terrible feeling in my stomach. It was a feeling I'd get before taking a test or going to a party where I don't know most of the kids. Anyway, it was a rotten feeling. I passed the Garden of Eden bungalows. They looked like a mining town that had been through an outlaw raid. There wasn't a sign of any people, just broken windows and pieces of furniture all over the place. I figured the place was ready for the bulldozer.

The B-L-U on the sign BLUE CHANNEL DAY CAMP shone with a new coat of paint. I sat on the boardwalk railing with my back toward the ocean and watched the sign painter drink coffee. I guess I must have made him uncomfortable, because he gulped down the coffee and went back to work on the sun-faded E.

I thought about jobs and wondered what it would be like to spend the rest of my life as a sign painter. The whole idea of jobs seemed pretty crummy to me. My father was always complaining about his job and boss. He was always saying how he didn't get paid enough, or how tired he always got. I wasn't too sure about what I wanted to do when I grew up. But I figured I had to do something where no one would boss me around, and maybe travel to different places.

I turned and looked at the ocean. The fishing boats were out, and I tried to imagine what it would be like to be a fisherman. I just wanted to run. I opened the top button of my shirt and took a deep breath. I tried to think about the plus side of getting the job, so it would be a little easier when I walked in there. I thought about the extra money, and getting myself a new bathing suit. I thought about how if I did get the job it would make my mother and father kind of happy. I walked to the camp entrance and went in.

Water was slowly trickling into a swimming pool painted sky blue. Irwin was nailing a rubber pad to a low diving board. He waved to me with the hammer in his hand. Then he ran over to me and said, "Hey, I'm glad you came. Myra said you wouldn't."

All I could say was, "Myra doesn't know everything."

"Come on," he said. "I'll introduce you to Stanley, he's head man around here."

I followed Irwin to a small white building with a sign OFFICE over it. I hated offices, and especially in the summer they seemed so unnatural.

The man inside looked like at one time he might have been a great athlete. He was big and sort of balding. He was wearing a sweat shirt with the name of the camp on it. When he saw Irwin he smiled. I didn't like him right away, because he seemed like the type of guy that would just like a kid if he was good at sports, and not care if he was really a louse.

He put aside whatever he was doing and sat on the edge of his desk and lit up a pipe. The more I looked at him, the more he reminded me of a coach that tells his team to go in and win, and they win for him.

"This is the kid I was telling you about," said Irwin.

The guy put out his hand, and with his pipe locked into his mouth said, "Stanley Morgan's the name."

I was sure happy he said his name first. I said "Hello, I'm Gordon Cassman." I didn't know what else to say, and my mother's dumb speech, what I remembered of it, would just seem out of place.

"Irwin's told me a lot about you," he said, trying to get a good draw on his pipe. The office became filled with a rotten-smelling tobacco—it smelled like old socks burning. I tried not to breathe, and when I finally did take a deep breath, he said, "You like the smell? It's my own mixture."

I looked down at his feet to see if he was wearing socks. He wasn't. Then he went into a whole thing about how poor the camp was and how they almost didn't open this year, and how they don't have money to fix the leaky pool. He also said, "You understand we can't pay too much, and you are inexperienced."

I wanted to ask him why he bothered opening up, and I also figured he wanted me to say, "I'll work for nothing."

He tapped the ashes out of his pipe into an empty tomato juice can that was on his desk. He looked up and said. "So if you want the job, Gordie, it's yours."

"Big deal," I said to myself. "Nobody else wants it! I'm sure he couldn't give it away."

For some reason I said, "Yes." And the more I thought about it, the more the "some reason" was my mother. It was important to her.

"Welcome aboard," he said, and he put his hand on my shoulder. I suddenly felt myself get tight. I'd seen guys like him around before, and I always stayed away from them because they talked score talk, and also because I felt that if they found out I wasn't the greatest on a ball field they'd really ride me. That's one reason I hung around with Larry—because he never talked ball scores like so many of the kids did.

A tall guy with a baseball cap came into the office. "The lockers are all in shape," he said.

"Mel, this is Gordie," said Mr. Stanley.

I said, "Hello."

"How's your pitching arm?" he asked.

Right then I wanted to run out and say, "This whole thing is a great big mistake!" But I didn't. I just smiled and shrugged my shoulders.

9

A CASE OF THE SIGHS

When I got back to Steiner's, I saw a familiar pair of sneakered feet hanging over the porch of our old bungalow. It was Larry.

"What's the hurry?" he called out.

Larry was sitting with a real dumb-looking kid who was in the wheelchair. He had casts on both his legs, and Larry had already gotten to them with his Magic Markers. Picking up my reaction to the casts, Larry laughed. "He's a member of the group. Gordie, I'd like you to meet a buddy of mine. This is Harold."

I said, "Hello," and the kid just smiled a nutty kind of smile. He drooled a little from his mouth and nose.

I didn't want to tell Larry about the job. I figured he'd know soon enough, and I could almost hear the baloney he'd hand me when I told him. I also had some kind of guilty feeling, like I was running out on him.

"This is Harold's dollhouse," said Larry. "Harold plays with the dollhouse, doesn't he?"

Larry spoke the way I remembered kids did when they read from their first-grade reader.

"Nice meeting you, Harold," I said, feeling kind of stupid. Because all Harold did was give me another crazy smile and drool a little more from his mouth.

I wondered if Harold was part of a long-range project for Larry or some quickie kind.

"What do you have, a hot date?" Larry asked after sizing up my shirt and tie outfit.

"Yeah!" I said, running off to tell my mother about the job.

I ran into the bungalow and the screen door slammed closed.

"How many times must I tell you not to slam the door!" my mother said, half shouting.

"I got the job," I said.

"That's nice," she said. "Have you seen the spaghetti strainer?"

I shook my head no. It suddenly seemed as if my mother couldn't have cared less about me getting the job or not. I had just given my summer away to make her a little happy and all she could ask about was her stupid spaghetti strainer. I could only think that it was all part of her changes.

"Maybe you left the strainer at home," I said.

"Don't tell me I left it at home!" she said, almost annoyed. "I know I took it, because it meant not taking the big white soup pot."

"Spaghetti strainers don't disappear," I said, trying in a way to comfort her.

"Around here anything is possible," she said.

When Myra came home and I told her that I got the job, she said, "I knew it all the time."

And when my father heard about it, he said, "Now you'll have to work hard to prove yourself."

My father brought home a map of the Thousand Islands for my mother. And I just about felt like crawling under the floor when my mother sat with the maps at the table and said, "Which island do you think Steiner is on?"

The electric bulb with the plastic flowered shade that hung over the table made strange shadows around the room. Even with all the lights on in the bungalow, everything looked like you were seeing it from the last row in the balcony of a movie the-ater.

My mother pushed the map aside and continued her thing about the spaghetti strainer.

"You left it at home," said my father.

"Don't tell me that!" said my mother with a real bark to her voice.

"I'm sure it will turn up," said my father.

"It's most peculiar," said my mother.

"You'll find it, don't worry, you'll find it," said my father, who was trying to calm my mother, who I could tell was getting kind of edgy. "And if it doesn't turn up, we'll buy another one," he said, putting his arm around her waist.

"That's not the point," she said, shaking herself free from his hold.

My father changed the subject. "I came in on the train with Mr. Levenson, and he invited us over for a game of gin tonight."

I really wondered if my mother was going through a difficult time in her life or if it was just the bunga-low with its unsolved mystery of why Widow Kravitz left her hat there. I was almost positive my mother had convinced herself that Widow Kravitz had died in the bungalow. She didn't have to come out and say it, I just knew it. And I knew according to my mother's way of thinking it could only mean bad luck. It all seemed like bad timing, my mother's menopause thing and her being stuck in a bungalow that made her uneasy. I couldn't imagine them just packing up and leaving the bungalow after paying out all the money for it. I mean like my mother doesn't throw money away.

I felt pretty doomed myself, knowing that I had to start work at Blue Channel the next morning.

Myra had a date with Irwin and she was really worried about what she looked like. She had spent the whole day at the beach and she looked it.

"I look like a beet," said Myra.

"You look more like a stewed tomato," I laughed.

"No one, but absolutely no one appreciates your stupid humor," she said while she fussed with herself in front of the mirror.

Irwin picked Myra up and said something stupid to me, like, "We're glad to have you on our team, Gordie!" Sometimes Irwin's talk seems like bits and pieces of leftover conversations.

"Do you believe what I look like?" said Myra. "And I hurt too!"

I wondered if Myra was fishing for some compliment, because Irwin picked up on it and said, "You look great to me." Myra left smiling.

The bungalow was real warm, so I sat on the porch thinking I would cool off. But it was just as hot outside.

"Boy, it's a hot night," I could hear my father tell my mother.

"I think we'll have to invest in an electric fan," said my mother. She sighed real heavy.

I didn't know if it was just the heat, but it seemed to me my mother sighed a lot more lately. It was something I'd seen old Widow Kravitz do a lot.

"I hope this summer wasn't a mistake," she said.

"What kind of mistake?" said my father. "You're here at the beach with the kids. Didn't you have a good time last summer?"

"Last summer and this summer are two different things," said my mother.

"They sure are!" I said to myself.

"Betty, everything is going to be fine, you'll see. You'll feel better in no time at all," said my father. "Come, let's get to the Levensons' for a game of gin."

There was an awfully long silence and I sort of held my breath until my mother answered, "Okay, I'll get ready." She sighed again.

I couldn't help but wonder if Widow Kravitz left her sighs in the bungalow also.

10

DEVIL FACE

"Gordon Cassman, you are wanted by the League." I would have to be a real retard not to have recognized Larry's voice and line of patter. I also knew he was probably hiding under the porch.

"The League of Crappy Doo Doo," I said in an equally dumb voice.

"I've warned you before—don't make fun of the League," he continued in his same crazy voice.

"I am sorry but I am not a follower," I said, trying to mimic him.

"That's what you think," said Larry, jumping up onto the porch and talking in his natural voice.

"Where's your new friend?" I asked, wanting to get Larry off of his demon topic.

Larry knew right away who I was asking about, but he pretended for a few minutes that he didn't know. Then he said, "Oh, backward boy. He has to go to bed at seven thirty. Boy, are we going to have some laughs with him this summer. Do you know, his mother told me that he broke his legs trying to roller-skate?" Larry laughed loud.

For some dopey reason it was hard for me to tell Larry about the job. I mean, it was as if I was doing something wrong by taking it. It seemed like I was leaving him without anyone to hang around with all summer. I'm really lousy when it comes to telling someone something straight off.

My mother and father came out onto the porch. They said hello to Larry. Then my mother said to me, "Remember, Gordie, tomorrow's a working day, so try to get to bed early." I watched my father sort of support my mother as they walked down the sandy path to the Levensons' bungalow.

"What's this about a working day?" Larry asked.

"Would you believe I've got a job?" I said. Then I went into a whole thing about the job and how I got conned into it. I played up that part especially big.

I was right about what Larry's reaction would be.

76

He said, "That sounds great, being with all those little kids all day."

"I'm not running out on you, Larry," I said. "First of all, I don't work nights and I don't work weekends."

At the same time I was trying to convince Larry that we'd still buddy around, it sounded as if I was trying to tell myself that the job wouldn't be too bad.

"Come on, let's go on the boardwalk," I said, trying in some way to cheer Larry up.

The smell of hot dogs and potato knishes was really strong on the boardwalk. And you could tell by the number of red faces that a lot of people had spent their time in the sun.

All the places on the boardwalk were open. Most of the places from last year were the same, but Mitzi's Souvenir Shop was now a bookstore, with a big sign in front: NO ONE UNDER TWENTY-ONE ADMITTED.

"They sell dirty books," said Larry. "Boy, I'd sure like to get my hands on some."

"Yeah, but how can we get in there?" I said, because I wanted to see them also.

We hung around in front of the store for a while and looked at the magazines they had in the windows, but all the good parts were taped over. They had magazines of men and women.

We stayed around as if we were going to turn twenty-one at the sound of some bell. While we were there, the new Lonesome Pete walked out of the store with a magazine rolled under his arm. He looked at Larry and me, and he smiled what seemed to me an embarrassed kind of smile. Then he said, "Hi, boys!"

I smiled back so he wouldn't feel as if his smile was stupid and wasted. Larry said, "Boy, that guy could be on TV!" He added, with envy in his voice, "I'll bet he makes out like crazy!"

"I suppose so," I said. If it was true, I wondered why he was buying dirty books.

The boardwalk was a whole different scene from the night before, and from the morning. Each time it was like a different place.

The glass dome of Luna Land glowed from inside, making it look almost like some kind of cathedral.

We passed the same tough girls we had seen the night before, and Larry said, "They're really looking for action." But he made no attempt to get their attention. And I wasn't about to, because they really scared me. Especially since I remembered some of their boyfriends from last year. I guess Larry must have sensed my wondering why he was so cool if he was really interested in making out. So I think it was for my benefit that he made a dumb sound for them to hear—it was the kind of noise you make when calling a cat or dog.

"Boy, you're going to miss all the action," he said.

"What action?"

"The action that happens under the boardwalk during the day."

I didn't know if he was trying to feed me a line of garbage and make me feel bad about having the job, or if he was really onto something that I didn't know about. It was hard to tell with Larry.

"You're full of crap," I said.

"I heard about it from one of the lifeguards, honest," he said. "There's this place near Luna Land—it's sort of right under Fatty's Pizza Place. Well, I heard all last summer these girls from Bath Beach were making it there with the lifeguards."

"During the day? Under the boardwalk?" I said.

"Yeah, during the day, under the boardwalk."

"Good for them!" I said, really wishing I could see for myself the next day. If Larry had intended to do what I thought he wanted to do, it worked. I suddenly hated the idea of going to work more than ever. I really felt as if I was going to miss out on a good time.

I pictured myself surrounded by little kids all summer, not even getting near the dirty book store or seeing the action under the boardwalk. I really envied Larry and his having a rich father. I mean like he'd never have to ruin a summer by working.

The people-sounds on the boardwalk were drowned out by the laughing lady in front of the Crazy House. The laughing lady was a big mechanical dummy who had the weirdest laugh going, and no matter how many times I saw her she really broke me up.

She was dressed differently from what I remembered from last year. But she was still wild-looking with her crazy hat and her big pair of men's shoes painted gold.

When I looked at her for a while and listened, I got the feeling that there was someone inside of her trying to break loose. I imagined my mother going completely crazy and ending up inside a big dummy like this.

Last year I also made a crazy lady puppet that really broke the kids up. I thought about making another one. I almost felt as if Larry was reading my thoughts when he said, "I suppose you'll be making puppets and putting on shows for the little kids."

I didn't want to give him a direct answer so I said, "Who knows?"

I knew he knew that's probably what I'd end up doing, and when he found out for sure he'd ride me about playing with dolls or some crap like that.

As we walked toward Luna Land, Larry got kind of quiet. He broke the quiet by saying, "My father might be getting married to some airline stewardess. I met her; she's young enough to be his daughter. I guess there's plenty of action left in my old man."

I didn't know what to say, but I felt bad for Larry, because I knew he had hoped his mother and father would get back together. He always said they were just on a trial separation.

The only thing I could say to cheer him up, and myself as well, was, "I'll probably get fired from the job anyway. What do I know about being a junior counselor?"

Heat lightning flickered in the sky, and then all you could hear was long *ooooohhh's* from the people along the boardwalk. It was like they expected something terrible to happen.

Larry stopped in front of a souvenir shop that

had rows of masks strung across the window. He looked for a long time.

"What are you looking at?" I asked him.

He put his finger on the window as if to touch the mask in front of him.

"I'm looking at myself," he said. His finger rested on a devil's mask.

II

THE CAT VISITOR

When I got back to the bungalow I had a real uneasy feeling. I don't know if it had something to do with no one's being there, or Larry's dumb devil remark, or even about starting work the next morning. Maybe it was all three. Anyway, it was an unexplainable feeling that made me kind of jumpy.

I was wishing in a way that my mother and father or Myra would return soon. I thought about my dream, and in some crazy way I was almost sure that if I went from room to room and acted it out, an old lady all in black would follow me onto the porch.

For some dumb reason I began to hunt for my mother's spaghetti strainer. As I searched through the pots and pans I thought of how each one of them sort of had a personality. They were pots that I had seen used over and over again. There was the potato-boiling pot, and the frying pan for scrambled eggs. I remembered nursery tales where spoons would talk to forks and forks to plates. And an idea came to me about making a whole set of puppets that would be kitchen things. The more I thought about the idea, the more I liked it. Then I heard a cat crying and the whole puppet idea stopped.

I listened awhile and I heard the cat cry again. It sounded like it was almost in the bungalow. And I started the here-kitty-kitty routine, but the cat didn't show—it just kept crying. I went out on the porch and it stopped. Just as I was about to go inside again, I heard it, and it sounded like it was coming from under the porch. Just a few boards remained of the once-fancy latticework from around the underpart of the porch, so it didn't matter much that I moved a few more boards out of the way. I got on my hands and knees and looked into the blackness under the porch. A strong, musty smell filled my nose, making me almost dizzy. I began again with the here-kitty-kitty, and sure enough this scroungy old gray-and-white cat came up to me. I sat cross-legged under the porch and let the old cat rub itself against me, and it purred up a storm.

I sat there thinking how terrific animals are, and how we were never allowed to have any. My mother always said they made her nervous.

Myra and Irwin returned. I could hear them walk up the steps to the porch. I heard Myra call into the bungalow, "Anyone at home? I guess no one is here yet," she said.

Then I heard Irwin say, "Good!"

There was a long quiet, and I heard Myra say, "Irwin, come on, cut it out."

Irwin said, "Well, we're practically going steady."

"You boys are all alike," Myra laughed.

I sat quietly and wondered what they were doing. I knew Myra wasn't like the girls under the boardwalk. Well anyway, in my mind she couldn't be, because she was my sister. It's kind of dumb, but if I like someone real well, I might know they're up to no good, but I find it hard to let myself believe it. Just like when I don't like someone, I just won't allow myself to think anything good about them. Myra sometimes says I have a closed mind.

I jumped up with the cat in my arms. "Look what I found!" I said.

"Oh God!" screamed Myra. "You scared the daylights out of me."

Irwin looked shook also. You didn't have to be

too smart to know what they'd been up to. Anyway, Irwin gave it away when he began to wipe Myra's Primrose Dawn lipstick off of his face.

I could tell Myra was embarrassed. I was also, for both of them.

"Where did you get that thing from?" she asked, with a nervous edge to her voice.

"It was crying under the porch, so I hunted it out."

Irwin stood around looking kind of dumb. Then he left with an excuse exit line about being in tip-top shape for the kids tomorrow.

"Where are you going with that thing?" Myra said as I took the cat into the bungalow with me. "If Mother catches you, you've had it."

She untied a ribbon from her hair and shook it loose. Myra looked pretty and she had a secret kind of smile on her face.

I knew Myra had tucked her blouse in extra tight before Irwin picked her up. And I knew that she knew she looked kind of sexy.

I watched the cat lick up the milk I gave it. It disappeared in a hurry. Sometimes Myra can be real tight-lipped, but I could tell from the mood she was in that she wouldn't mind talking to me. And she wouldn't end every sentence with, "You're too young to understand," or "I don't know why I bother."

"Did you have fun?" I asked.

Myra's hair fell over one eye, and with one hand on her hip and one hand pulling her hair away from her face, she said in a funny, sexy way, "I always have fun."

I laughed. I fed the cat more milk and Myra went into her room. I lay down on my bed and let the cat rest on my chest. After a while Myra came out in her bathrobe. She sat down and began to brush her hair. "I wonder if I should go steady with Irwin?"

I knew Myra wasn't talking to me. She was talking to herself and I just happened to be there. Anyway I didn't say anything. I just listened to the cat purring.

Myra continued talking. "The summer is just beginning. I don't want to rush into things."

I knew before she went to bed that night Myra would write all about it in her diary.

Myra stopped talking and looked at the cat. "That silly cat looks like it's wearing a gray wig."

"You're right!" I laughed, looking at the cat's face. "It almost looks like Widow Kravitz."

"It's a good thing Mother isn't here to hear that," said Myra. "She'd have a fit."

I figured this was as good a time as any to pin

87

Myra down. "Do you think Mother's changes are driving her crazy?" I asked.

Myra looked at me very seriously for a moment, then she looked at her brush as if it was going to give her some answer. "Mother's change of life could be causing her a traumatic experience." She put her brush down. "Mother is definitely experiencing something," she said.

The "experiencing something" made me wonder if my mother might be having one of her feelings like something was going to happen, only this time it was going to be terrible. Or whether her jumpy behavior was because of her woman's problems that were aggravated by us being in Widow Kravitz's bungalow.

I asked Myra this, and she said, "I don't know. I've thought about it, but I really don't know."

She came over to me and picked the cat off of my chest. And then in sort of a baby-talk way, Myra said, "And how is little pussy cat?"

"Meow," I said. "Would you please scratch my head?"

Myra looked right at the cat and pretended it had spoken. "No, little cat, I'll not scratch your head—I might upset your little gray wig."

Then Myra sat at the table and played with the cat. "Gordie, everything is going to be all right. You'll see."

I think Myra was trying to convince herself as well as me. She looked kind of different with her pink robe and her hair hanging loose. If someone had asked me what color Myra's hair was, I would have answered "brown." But now looking at it with the kitchen light directly above her it wasn't just brown, it was golden brown. The cat jumped up on Myra's lap, and she looked at me and smiled. Myra was really very pretty, even though she was still wearing her Sultry Night eye makeup and her Primrose Dawn lipstick. I couldn't understand why so many girls needed that stuff. In Myra's case I think it was almost like a security blanket. She sure knew how to load it on.

Myra bent down to let the cat off of her lap, and her bathrobe opened a little on top, and I could see where her sunburn ended.

I thought about the dirty book store, and how I could get in there. If Myra got all dressed up I wondered if they would let her in the store and wouldn't question her age. I couldn't ask Myra to get me a dirty book, although I was tempted to bring the subject up. I really wanted one. I thought about the under-the-boardwalk action I was going to miss, and I hated the idea of going to work even more.

"Come here, cat." Myra stood at the front door holding it open, hoping to coax the cat into leaving.

"What are you doing?" I jumped up.

"What does it look like I'm doing?" said Myra. "The cat has to go before Mother gets home."

I knew Myra was right but I hated to see the cat leave.

"It's not like it's winter," said Myra. She bent down and picked the cat up and held it next to her for a while before she put it on the porch.

"Anyway, it probably belongs to someone."

"Do you think it's a he or a she?" I said, wanting to grab the cat and bring it inside one more time.

"Stop being such a jerk," said Myra, and she slammed the door shut. "What difference does it make anyway?" she said.

"Well, it might to its friends," I said.

Myra gave me one of her famous "Oh God, you poor idiot!" looks.

I asked Myra if she had seen the retarded kid in our old bungalow, and she told me she had.

"I feel sorry for him in a way," I said.

"I feel sorry for his parents," said Myra.

"I feel sorry for me going to work tomorrow."

"Do you know, when you think about it, it's one of the worst things you can do for someone," said Myra.

"What's that?" I asked.

"To feel sorry for them."

I sort of knew what Myra meant.

Myra started sniffing her bathrobe, at the shoulder part where she'd held the cat. "That's strange," she said.

"What's strange?" I asked.

"Well, where I held the cat, it smells like Widow Kravitz. It smells like her hat did this morning."

I didn't even have to go close to Myra to know what she was talking about. I just took a deep breath and a lemony tea smell filled my head.

I felt a sudden chill.

12

THE PHONE CALL

It was real early when I started out for camp. I walked along the beach. The ocean was quiet. I watched some gulls ripping apart a fish. From the clock on the frankfurter billboard I could tell that I had plenty of time before I was to report for my first day at work.

Whenever I have something important to do, even if it's something I don't really like, I always make sure I'm early. I just hate being late for anything. But I go to extremes about being early. I was out of the bungalow before anyone was up. And I didn't feel like eating breakfast either.

When my mother was at the Levensons' the night

before, they convinced her that Mr. Steiner was in California visiting his son. Mrs. Levenson said that she thought his son lived in Encino, California. My mother said that she was going to call him today. She asked me where I had heard the Thousand Islands story from, and I told her I couldn't remember. I was happy about my mother's discovery— first of all I was sorry I ever made the dumb story up, because it really made me uncomfortable to see my mother poring over those stupid maps, and I hoped now that the situation would be cleared up in some way.

The more I looked at the ocean, the more I got the feeling that I wanted to run in. So I took off my shoes and socks and ran into the water.

My feet sank into the wet sand, and the cold water around my ankles almost hurt. Far out on the ocean I could see the gray outline of a big ship. I always figured all big ships go to foreign countries. And if ever there was a time I felt like being on one, this was it. I didn't really feel like facing up to Morgan Stanley or Stanley Morgan and his pipe-face scene.

I kept tossing shells into the ocean, and the more I thought about working, the madder I got. If only Irwin wasn't working there, I could make up a story about them not needing me and it was all a big mistake. Everything this summer seemed like a big mistake.

The Blue Channel Day Camp sign had a new coat of paint, but it really looked lousy. Underneath, you could still see where the old paint had been peeling.

I hung around outside until I saw Irwin with the kid Mel and a girl I didn't know. Irwin and Mel said, "Hello," and they introduced me to the girl. Her name was Arlene and she was a counselor for the girls. She looked okay. She was wearing a man's shirt that she tied up on top so that you could see her whole middle including her belly button.

Stanley Morgan came out of his office with his pipe firmly stuck in his mouth. I had a feeling he thought the pipe made him seem real cool. There were some other counselors hanging around and it seemed like everyone knew each other. I didn't know anyone except Irwin, and he wasn't paying any attention to me. It also seemed like everyone was clued in on something that I wasn't. I just felt like I didn't belong. But I get that feeling most of the time anyway.

Pipe-face Morgan blew a whistle to get everyone's attention, and schoolyard pictures passed in front of me. He told the staff to quiet down and he said this was going to be a quickie meeting before the children arrived.

It was hard for me to pay attention to him, because when he spoke it really sounded like he was just listening to himself. So he just didn't reach me. I did hear him say things like "Safety for the children," and words like "Responsibility," and "No goofing off," and "Setting good examples."

The water level in the pool hadn't changed any from the day before—it was just one big useless cement sky-blue hole.

I didn't know if pipe-face Morgan saw me looking at the pool or if that was his next topic but he said, "Until the pool is repaired we'll do our swimming in the ocean!" That was really okay with me.

Then he went back to safety talk. Irwin whispered to me, "They don't have money to fix the pool. As a matter of fact, they don't have too much money for anything."

The kids started arriving and I was sort of happy to see Avram Hurwitz and Dee Dee Levenson among them.

The meeting broke up and we were assigned to our groups. Avram was in mine, and he put his arm around my waist and hugged me. I liked Avram. When you first saw him you'd say he was an ugly kid, but when he smiled it was a whole different thing.

The day was spent getting a buddy system for swimming, and trying to set up some kind of nature and arts-and-crafts corner. We also hung a net up for a really uninspired game of volleyball, with probably one of the world's worst volleyballs. It had been repaired so many times it almost resembled Frankenstein's head.

The first day really dragged, with most of the time spent trying to find things for the kids to do. Aside from it being poor, Blue Channel wasn't exactly the most organized place in the world. If I had a kid I wouldn't send him there.

When the last kid left and the camp day was finally over, I really felt beat. Pipe-face Morgan called me over and asked what I thought it would cost for the kids to make puppets. I told him not too much. All we needed was paper and paste for the papier-mâché and bits of cloth for costumes. He thought it would be a good idea if we got a project like that started. I must admit I responded with some enthusiasm.

I walked home along the boardwalk, and the new Lonesome Pete had already begun to work. If he had a good voice you sure couldn't tell from the rotten amplifying system the Texas Bar had hooked up.

I watched him sing for a while. He saw me, and he winked and smiled. I wished I could take a look at his dirty magazines. Then I thought if I could only get to know him and I gave him the money, he could buy some for me. The more I thought about it the more it seemed like it might be a good idea. I mean he seemed nice enough, like he always smiled, and maybe sometime he would do me a favor. I thought about a good hiding place for them—it was going to be hard in the bungalow.

I had almost forgotten that my mother had planned on contacting Mr. Steiner that day, and when I got back to the bungalow my mother was really irritable.

"Could you imagine?" she said. "I called all the way to Encino, California, and Steiner's daughter-in-law answers the phone and tells me Mr. Steiner just left for Disneyland with his grandchildren. It was like throwing good money down the toilet. Now I'll have to make another call."

Myra was the only one who asked me how the first day went. I told her okay.

After supper I waited on the front porch for my

mother, who was busy counting her tons of change for her next call to California. She wanted me to go with her when she made the call.

Larry came by, wheeling Harold in his chair. For some reason, Larry got the confidence of Harold's mother, and all and all, it seemed like Larry was playing good guy, which he might have been. But knowing Larry, I figured there had to be another reason for his interest in this retarded kid.

The kid looked extra dumb with his legs stretched out on the wheelchair and Larry's decorations all over his casts. In a way he looked like he could have almost been related to Laughing Lady at the Crazy House.

"How's Satan and his son?" I asked.

Larry didn't answer. Harold waved a little doll's bed at me, one that must have come from the big dollhouse.

"Bed," Harold said, kind of drooling all over himself.

"Bed, go to sleep," said Larry in a crazy infant way, almost mimicking Harold.

Then Larry said, "They should have put this kid to sleep when he was born."

It suddenly seemed like Larry was a murderer talking. Then I looked at Harold real hard, and for some reason I began to wonder if Larry might have been right. I thought it was terrible of me to even think that, and at the same time I just couldn't push it out of my mind.

"Well, did you get fired today?" Larry asked.

"Come off it," I said. "No, I didn't get fired!"

Then as if to justify my sticking with the job, I said, "Anyway I need the money."

"It's too bad you got all screwed up this summer with that job, especially when I'm beginning to get connections with the under-the-boardwalk scene."

"Sure, sure!" I said, not really knowing whether to believe Larry or not. "You can't even get to the dirty book store," I said, hoping Larry would come back with some kind of plot or answer about getting in there.

But he didn't. He just said, "See you around," and he wheeled Harold toward the boardwalk.

My mother came out of the bungalow with change rattling in a brown paper bag. "Come quick," she said, "before Markey's closes."

Markey's Appetizing Store was just about to close when my mother put on this tremendous act about she had to use the phone for an emergency. "A sister of mine is very sick," said my mother. I really felt embarrassed for my mother and her lying routine.

"Gordie, you get the number for me," she said, handing me the bag of change.

The phone smelled of fish and it had some fish scales stuck to it. I hated the idea of using it. While I was dialing, it suddenly hit me that my mother's whole purpose of contacting Steiner all the way out in California to find out if Widow Kravitz died in the bungalow was really insane. I finished dialing and handed the phone to my mother. She grabbed at it like a hungry gull.

I wanted to say, "Momma forget it, it's all so silly!" But before I had a chance to say anything she was on the phone with Mr. Steiner. After she asked him what she wanted, she shouted back into the phone.

"I don't believe you!" she said. "I don't believe you!"

"Mother, please," I said. I took the phone from her and hung it up.

"I know he lied to me," said my mother. "I could just feel it. He said she left the bungalow in perfectly good health. And he said he wished he had his records with him so that he could give me her address. But you know what? I don't believe him."

Mr. Markey was looking at my mother and I felt bad. It seemed like my mother was really disappointed to hear that Widow Kravitz was alive and well.

"Why would he lie?" I said.

"Because he was afraid I'd ask for my money back. No one wants to spend a summer in a bungalow where someone died."

When we got back to the bungalow my father was there, and I was glad. My mother went into the whole thing about how Steiner was lying to her and maybe we should pack up and leave. My father spoke to my mother for a long time, and whatever he told her seemed to work, because she was calm afterward.

Late that night my father said to me, "Gordie, try to understand. Your mother is going through a difficult time in her life, but everything will be all right soon." At the same time I'm sure he was trying to convince himself.

All I said was, "I know, Dad."

But I really had mixed feelings about everything. In the phone booth the whole thing about reaching Steiner seemed really crazy. But back in the bungalow things seemed different. It was something I couldn't explain to myself. It just seemed like there might be some reason for my mother's actions.

13

THE PROJECT

The next day at camp I was almost happy to be there. Part of it might have been selfish—I was glad to be away from the bungalow and my mother. But another reason was that Stanley Morgan brought in all the stuff for the puppets. He called me over and dumped the whole thing on me. "Your project," he said.

A few days passed and I became known as Project Puppet around the camp. I found myself not minding it too much. It meant that I was excused from all activities except swimming, and it was fun for me because the kids really liked doing it.

A lot of the counselors yelled at the kids, but I

didn't—I guess only because I can't stand being yelled at myself.

The nature corner was mostly seashells until one red-headed kid brought in a crippled bird he found on the beach. He said he wanted to keep it when it got better. And I began to take care of it. It almost seemed hopeless at first, but then I fed it with an eye-dropper and it began to come around.

We went swimming every afternoon, and when we got back to the camp we showered. The kids showered before the counselors.

One afternoon after the kids left and I was shower-ing, I rubbed myself with the towel and began to arouse myself. Irwin noticed and grabbed my towel away. I felt like crawling through the drain.

"Hey, look what Gordie's got!" he shouted. The other counselors laughed. I was really embarrassed as all hell, and Irwin knew it, and right after he did it I could tell he was sorry.

Afterward he made sure that he walked out of the shower with me. "Gee, Gordie, I'm sorry," he said. "It happens to me all the time, usually just when I have to get off of a bus or stand up."

I laughed. "It happens a lot to me then, too."

There was talk around camp about the possibility

of having a carnival with different games of skill and chance. And sort of half joking, I said, "Why don't we put on a puppet show also?"

Arlene was quick on the uptake, and she suggested that we advertise the carnival and puppet show and put up posters along the boardwalk. "And charge admission, of course," she said.

Everyone thought it was a terrific idea. I began to think of a good show idea to put on. Stanley Morgan told me I was a great thinker.

I felt guilty about my first impression of him, because he was really a nice guy.

There seemed to be a calm at the bungalow, but I could almost feel that it was a temporary thing. I mean like my mother was just too quiet.

Myra complained to me about her baby-sitting job during the day and said that the kid she had to mind was a real brat who was sending her up the wall. Sometimes Myra baby-sat at night also, but I knew she didn't mind that because Irwin baby-sat with her. And from all indications they were unofficially going steady.

I told Myra about the carnival idea and the puppet show. She already knew about it from Irwin, who had told her that all the kids were nuts about me. It really made me feel great, I mean like it was really important.

I tried to sound out Myra about what she thought would be a good show to put on. Myra was good when it came to things like that. She knows all about movies, shows and songs.

She said we should choose something children and adults would like. I couldn't think of anything— my mind was a real blank. But then Myra came up with what seemed like a sensational idea.

"It's a natural, an absolute natural," she said.

"Well, how about letting me in on it?" I said.

She laughed. "Put on *The King and I*."

At first I told her she had to be kidding, but the more I thought about it, the more it seemed like a really good idea.

"I could kiss you," I said. I felt silly afterward because I realized the last time I kissed Myra was when we were little.

I knew it was going to be a big job getting all the puppets made and costuming them, getting scenery built and teaching the kids how to work them. I figured the kids could do the speaking parts, and we'd use the show album for the musical parts.

I had learned my puppet-making from library

books, and I decided that I'd make do-it-yourself instruction books for the kids. I remembered those books well—it was almost as if they were a permanent part of my brain. But that part of the project I'd have to do in the bungalow.

When I started work on the kitchen table, my mother screamed and said I was making a mess of everything. And she told me I should quit the camp if that's what the job meant. I couldn't wait until my mother was all right again.

I talked to Myra about it, and she said, "We've just got be strong, Gordie."

I really felt as if my mother was turning into someone I didn't know, or didn't want to know.

The floor of the porch became my working table.

"How's the junior counselor?" Larry said, resting his elbows on the porch railing.

"Hi, Larry!" He sort of took me by surprise. I really didn't want him to see what I was working on.

"Oh, no!" he said. "Are you still fooling around with dolls?"

"They're not dolls, and—" I was just about to go into a long explanation, and then I just said, "Forget it."

"Speaking of dolls, you should see what I met. And I have a feeling we're going to be going all the way. The action on the beach is unbelievable!"

When Larry spoke about girls as dolls it was like he was talking from some script of a rerun TV show. I wondered if Larry thought about me wondering how come I never saw him with any girls. I mean I knew Larry wasn't stupid, so I'm sure it must have come into his head more than once.

I had the feeling that Larry was having a rotten summer and I felt a little responsible. It's not that I'm the greatest buddy someone can have, but I was sure that I was more fun than the retarded kid Harold.

"I can fix you up," said Larry, "if you're not afraid?"

"With what?" I said, "A mental retard?"

"You know, Gordie boy, sometimes I really think you're afraid of girls."

I wanted to come out and say the same thing to Larry, but I held it in. And anyway, Larry was right about me. I was really inexperienced. I thought a lot about the day it would all happen, but I wasn't too sure how you make it happen.

I figured one of these days I was going to go under the boardwalk.

14

FOUR FOR A QUARTER

"Shh, Mother's sleeping," said Myra.

Myra was sitting on the porch reading when I got home from camp.

"I'm not sleeping," said my mother.

I looked through the window that opened out onto the porch and I saw my mother lying on my bed. She had a washcloth across her forehead and a bowl of melting ice cubes was nearby on the floor.

"Who can sleep with these headaches?" she said.

My mother, who had always gone to the beauty parlor, no longer went. It was a long time since she had fixed her hair. She had taken to wearing it just brushed straight back. And when Myra said she'd help my mother fix her hair, my mother said, "For who, for what?" She didn't even go to the beach.

It made me feel lousy to see my mother this way. I guess Myra was able to read the worried look on my face, and she asked me how the puppets were coming.

I told her how Avram and Dee Dee had a big argument as to who'd be Anna's son and who would be the oldest prince. And I still wasn't too sure who wanted to be what.

Myra laughed. "That's kids for you. Do you remember when we were little and I played house, you never wanted to be my son, you always wanted to be the father."

Myra and I laughed. "What are you two kids laughing about?" my mother asked.

"We were just remembering silly things," I said.

"Don't lie, you were probably laughing about me," said my mother.

Myra and I looked at each other. Myra shook her head and I could see her eyes water up. She whispered, "I know it must sound selfish, but I wish I was old enough to get married."

I knew how Myra felt, because at times like this I wanted to run away. I was almost afraid to go inside the bungalow, because I thought I might get my mother started off on something else.

Myra suggested that I make supper, but she put down my idea of a tuna fish omelette. My mother stayed on my bed and I refilled the bowl with ice cubes, which she put on her head with the washcloth. She complained that the bungalow was stifling, and when we told her to go out for a walk, or to just sit on the porch, she said it was just as bad outside. Supper was tuna fish salad sandwiches that Myra loaded down with plenty of onions.

It was still light when I got to the boardwalk, and I was just about to make a wish on the first star, but I didn't when I noticed more than one star out. I sometimes think I'm nuts, but whenever I get a chance I make a wish on the first star. So far none of them ever happened. I really wanted to make a wish too. I wanted to wish that everything was okay again with my mother.

The red and yellow lights of the **Texas Bar** went on, and so did the lamplights along the boardwalk. The blue mirrors looked purple, reflecting sunset color from the sky.

I saw Lonesome Pete sitting on a bench looking out toward the ocean. His guitar was in a case looking like a friend sitting on the bench with him. He looked up and saw me leaning against the boardwalk railing. He smiled and said, "Hello."

I sort of felt shy at first, but then I told him that I thought he was a better singer than the one last year. He laughed and said, "Thanks." And then he said, "He had some corny name like Lonesome Pete."

"That's the name!" I said, feeling guilty about calling this guy Lonesome Pete.

"Well, my name is Earl Whitmore," he said, and he put out his hand to shake mine.

"I'm Gordie Cassman," I said.

Then I told him that I thought he was good-looking enough to star in some TV series.

He turned away and it seemed like he kind of turned red and said, "Aw, come on!"

"No, I really mean it," I said. "Even Larry Perl said so."

He was tan and his blue eyes really looked extra blue.

I caught a whiff of the onions on my breath and I backed away. I felt like asking him outright if I gave him money for a magazine at the dirty book store, if he'd get one for me. But I couldn't get up the nerve, so I backed away and said, "I'll see ya!"

"Take care, Gordie," he said. And he picked up

111

his guitar and went into the Texas Bar. He sort of turned and looked at me. I covered my mouth with my hand and breathed into it, and just about knocked myself out with the smell. I wondered if he smelled the onions on my breath and thought I was some kind of creep.

I felt like brushing my teeth, but I didn't want to go back to the bungalow. After supper my mother said something about why do I always have to go out and why don't I just stay around the bungalow some nights. It was really hard to do, especially the way things were. And if I did stay there, my mother would get to picking on me after a while. I think she purposely wanted me there so she could pick on me. It wasn't just me though—it was Myra and my father too.

Larry and his father passed me on the boardwalk, and seeing me was like a signal for his father to say, "I've got to go now, Larry. I suppose you'll want to be with Gordie, anyway."

I suppose Larry knew like I did that his father was using my appearance as a cop-out. I had a feeling his father just visited him as a duty thing. He handed Larry some money and rubbed the top of his head and then walked off the boardwalk. He didn't even turn around to look back once. And I know Larry was waiting for it, because he kept looking at his father.

After we walked awhile together, he said, "My father is really getting married." Larry sounded desperate.

I asked Larry if he wanted to see the day camp, hoping it would take his mind off of his father, and I figured if I showed him where I was working and what was happening he wouldn't feel so left out.

The camp gate was open and the light was on in Stanley Morgan's office. "Hi, Gordie," he said, coming out of his office. "Can't keep away from those puppets, can you?"

I introduced him to Larry. When I took Larry in to where we were making the puppets he said, "How can you stand this crummy place, anyway?"

I pretended not to hear Larry and I held up some puppet heads. "This is going to be the King," I said, "and this is going to be Anna."

"Oh jeez, Anna Banana! When are you going to grow up?"

Larry was wearing his demon sneakers that he'd brightened up with more colors. I looked down at them and wanted to say something about growing up to him, but I figured he was upset about his father, so I didn't.

Then I started talking about Arlene, not because I wanted to, but because I thought maybe that's what Larry wanted to hear about. And I was right, because the dirty talk started right away.

He asked me questions like, "How big are her boobs?" and "Do you think she really puts out?"

"She's goes around sticking them in everyone's face," I said. "I guess she's kind of got hot pants." I really felt rotten talking about Arlene that way. I mean it was true about her showing off her boobs, but as far as I knew it just stopped at that. And even if other things were true, it just seemed awful of me to talk about her. I suddenly had the urge to kick myself in the butt for starting up the whole Arlene conversation in the first place.

Then I said I had a plan for getting the dirty books. When I wouldn't tell it, Larry got a little sore. I didn't blame him for that one. But I just didn't want to tell him my plan about getting Lonesome Earl Whitmore to get them for me. It's like I'm forever digging traps for myself.

"Come on, let's go to Bat-Away," said Larry.

I was happy for the suggestion. I said, "Good night," to Stanley Morgan and he said something about how great he thought the puppets were coming. Larry said he looked like a super jock creep. I told him that was my first impression, but he wasn't that way at all. "He's really a nice guy," I said.

Larry and I weren't the greatest athletes but we didn't mind going to Bat-Away with its automatic pitcher. I kind of liked it. And I think one of the reasons I liked it better than playing baseball at school was because there wasn't anyone there to ride the pants off of you if you struck out. And I had a feeling Larry felt the same way.

The automatic pitcher kept the balls coming fast and low, and I only missed hitting two out of the ten balls. Larry treated for the sodas afterward and we gulped them down.

Then we had a burping contest and I really let out with some good ones. Larry said I cheated. He accused me of farting at the same time. I told him he was full of crap, and we began to wrestle.

Now I know Larry is stronger than me, but I'm faster, so I got out of his grip and raced along the boardwalk until I was out of breath. Then I hid in a four-for-a-quarter photo booth. It was a dumb place to hide, because Larry spotted my feet under the curtain.

He came into the booth and grabbed my head in a hammer hold. Then he put a quarter in the slot and the machine began to work and take our pictures. All the time Larry is squeezing my head. For each picture there'd be a flash of light and right before the last picture, Larry gave me a wet kiss on my face. I pushed him away and he laughed real loud and said, "How does it feel to be kissed by a demon?"

"Terrific!" I said. "When do we go steady?"

When the pictures came out of the slot, I grabbed them before Larry did and I ripped them up. I ran away while Larry picked up the pieces of pictures.

My mother was sleeping in my bed when I got to the bungalow, so I got in with my father. Although it had been a while since my mother had mentioned anything about Widow Kravitz, in some way she was still there, all the same.

15

WHO KILLED THE KING?

My mother was sitting on the porch when I left for camp in the morning. She said to me, "How is everything going at camp, Gordie?"

I told her about the puppets and she said she would like to come and see the show. I was happy to see her in a better mood, and except for the dark circles under her eyes she seemed all right. But I was used to seeing her go in and out of moods, so I wasn't exactly rejoicing. I did hope though that she wouldn't slip back into some awful funk. I never knew what to do or say anymore around the bungalow without triggering off some terrible kind of reaction. And there was some explosion when my father suggested she see a doctor. I don't know what kind of doctor he had in mind. Anyway she turned on him and wouldn't speak to him for a couple of days. It wasn't hard to tell that my father was going through a rough time of it also. It almost seemed like menopause was more like an evil spell. I thought about Larry and his claims to be tied in with Satan, and wild ideas of me selling myself to the devil to free my mother filled my head.

No matter how much I tried to push it out of my mind, I still kept coming back to the time last summer when I saw Widow Kravitz without her wig and I stupidly spread the word. And then what we all did, and how she cursed us. No matter how much I reasoned with myself, I couldn't help but feel in some way what was happening was all a part of that. And like any minute I expected something to happen to me.

At camp nobody felt like working on the puppets, myself included. The days were really sweltering, and even going to the bathroom seemed like a big project. When we went swimming there weren't any waves—the ocean was like a pond.

One afternoon Myra came down to the part of the beach where the camp went swimming. She had the afternoon off and I guess she wanted to see Irwin.

But he got real mad when he saw her, because he said he was on duty when she tried to talk to him. And they had an argument because Myra took the whole thing personally. Even though Myra was my sister, Irwin was right. But sometimes girls just aren't understanding about things like that.

Stanley Morgan gave the camp a pep talk. The sweat was pouring off of him like someone dumped water over him, but he said that if we were going to have a carnival and a puppet show we'd all better get going and show some real enthusiasm.

Arlene spoke up and said, "But it's so hot!"

And then Stanley Morgan said something like, "What do you think, the whole world shuts down because of a heat spell?" He went on about how it's a good thing farmers and truckers didn't think like we did or else we'd all be starving to death. I got warmer just listening and watching him smoke a pipe. I really thought pipes should just be smoked beside some fireplace, like I'd seen on real corny Father's Day cards.

We all went back to the puppet and carnival project, and Dee Dee and Avram continued their argument about who was going to be the favorite prince and who was going to be Anna's son. For the first time I lost my temper and told them to shut up—it was too hot to argue. I also told them that there were other kids and just because they knew me it didn't mean they would get the parts they wanted.

"We're going to have auditions," I said. "And whoever is best for the part will get it." That didn't go over too well with them, and I knew they thought I was some kind of traitor.

The day the first puppet got all put together and dressed and I showed them how it worked, the kids went wild. It's funny with puppets. If you look at them long enough, like with a spotlight on them in a dark room, they seem to have a life of their own, and the more you watch them, the more real and independent of their strings they become. I know it's happened to me. That's how I think I got interested in them in the first place.

After they saw the first one in action, the kids worked extra hard getting some of the others put together.

I told my mother about the puppets and how terrific everyone thought they were and it really cheered her. My mother made spaghetti and meatballs one night, and she was beginning to act more regular. When it came time to pour the spaghetti into a strainer, I saw that my mother had one. I was afraid to ask where it had come from. I wondered if she had found the one she was missing or if she had bought a new one. When I asked Myra, she said that my father had found it in the apartment. I was happy it turned up again.

The heat spell hadn't broken and it was really hard sleeping at night, so I found myself getting to camp early and working on the puppets. I would also go to the nature corner and feed the crippled bird, who had healed. I could see that the bird seemed eager to get out of its cage, so one day I walked to the beach with it and set it free. It was really beautiful to see it get its freedom back. I was glad no one was around, because my eyes got watery.

That afternoon when we got back from the beach, Arlene came screaming out of the room where we were making the puppets. "Oh Gordie, something terrible has happened!" she sobbed. I ran to where the puppets were and I couldn't believe what I saw. All the puppets were pulled apart. At first I was mad, and then I wanted to cry and then came a sinking feeling. There were heads, arms and legs all over the place.

"Who the hell would do that?" said Irwin.

"Someone depraved," said Stanley Morgan.

"It almost looks like some kind of sacrifice," Arlene sobbed.

I picked up the head of the king and looked at it for a while. "Okay, who did it?" I said.

"Right now, who did it is not as important as getting them back together," said Stanley Morgan. "Don't worry, we'll get the culprit."

A few suspects came to mind, but I figured I'd better wait and let them show their hands before I accused anyone. And I swore all kinds of revenge.

16

SUNDAY, SWEET SUNDAY

"Come on," said my father. "It'll do you some good."

"If you leave me alone," said my mother, "it will do me more good."

It was Sunday, and my father and Myra and me stood around in our bathing suits trying to coax my mother into going to the beach with us. But the awful mood was back again. My mother still hadn't gone to the beach. At times she avoided the neighbors and at times she was friendly. They never said anything—it was like they understood. I felt ashamed at times. I knew they could hear her yelling about something. Sometimes it was at me. When that happened, I wished there was a back door to the place so that I could get out unseen.

My father said he'd stay with my mother, but she got real mad and said that she just wanted to be by herself. I could tell my father was upset but he said, "Come, children, let Mother rest."

It was like my mother was living with some secret and guarding it by not leaving the bungalow.

The beach was crowded with people from the bungalows and the rooming houses as well as people who just came down for the day. It was almost easy to tell them all apart. I wasn't that crazy about the beach on Sundays—it was noisy, and by the end of the day you were practically buried in garbage.

An old bedspread served as a beach blanket, and we had just put it down on what seemed like a good spot when a family with seven thousand kids set up their blanket next to us.

Myra and I walked to the water with my father. He began to talk about things like a person getting older, and about temporary changes in a person's life that may cause them to behave strangely. And how they themselves are having a difficult time, and everyone around them must be understanding. I couldn't understand why my father just didn't come right out and say the person he was talking about was my mother. I wondered if in his way he tried to pretend that it wasn't her. Anyway, Myra and I got the message. It was very clear.

My father looked real pale in his bathing suit. He looked like someone who'd been shut in for a long time. I kind of felt sorry for him. It seemed to me that he was missing out on fun kinds of things. I knew he didn't like his job. Once he said if he were given the chance he wouldn't make the same mistakes again. I couldn't help but wonder if he considered my mother one of his mistakes.

Myra screamed, "Oh, it's freezing!" when we got to the water's edge. But my father dove right in and I went in after him. "Come on in!" I shouted to Myra.

"The water is disgusting," she shouted. In a way she was right. I picked a cigarette wrapper off of my shoulder, and looked at all the muck that was floating around me.

"The ocean is like a bath today," laughed my father.

"A dirty one," I said, splashing some more garbage away from myself.

I ran to drag Myra into the water, but she screamed a lot and said, "I forgot my bathing cap—my hair will be a mess."

125

"Forget your hair," I said, trying to splash water at her. I chased her back to the blanket and we ran into Irwin with Arlene. I could tell right away that Myra was real upset. I mean like she didn't even say hello to Irwin.

Pretending she didn't care, Myra loaded herself up with some sweet-smelling suntan oil and said I should do the same.

"It's going to be a scorcher," she said.

When I told her I didn't want any of that smelly stuff on me, she took a handful and rubbed it on my back anyway.

The mother with all the kids next to us started unloading gigantic shopping bags full of food. I think they had enough food for the entire beach. She seemed like a nice lady and I envied them.

My father joined us and he grabbed a towel. His hair was dripping wet and curly.

"That was good," he said. "Anyone hungry?"

Myra and I shook our heads no. After my father rubbed himself with the suntan oil he stretched out, and in absolutely no time at all he was sleeping.

I didn't want to think about the puppets, but just lying on the beach with nothing to do, my head wasn't empty for long.

I thought about who might have done it, and why. I thought of Larry trying to get even with me for ripping up the photos from the other night. I even thought about Avram and Dee Dee, who I had yelled at. For some reason it was Larry who seemed like my prime suspect. It just seemed like the sort of thing he would do. I knew if I confronted Larry with it, he'd just deny it. The only thing I figured I could do is just be cool and wait, and hope in some way Larry would eventually give himself away. And when that time came, boy, would I think of some great revenge!

I lay on my stomach and watched the family next to me. The mother was really fat and the father was a skinny little runt of a man. I tried to imagine them in bed together. And I broke myself up.

Myra looked at me with her sunglasses resting on the tip of her nose. "Are you cracking up?" she asked.

I couldn't tell her what I thought was so funny, so I made up a story about how I was giving the kids next to us names and how the fattest kid looked like his name should be Rollo.

Myra laughed. "Poor Daddy, he must be exhausted to be able to sleep through all this."

"Wouldn't it be great," I said, "if when we got back to the bungalow, Mother's changes were all over with?"

"Yes," smiled Myra. "But it doesn't happen that way."

"How does it happen?" I asked.

"I don't know. I suppose it will go as gradually as it came. And anyway, with each woman it's a different story." A serious expression came across Myra's face, and I had a feeling that she was suddenly thinking about herself when that time in her life came.

The sun really beat down and I looked up at it. I saw all kinds of colors pass in front of my eyes. Terrific colors for the puppet show.

I went to the boardwalk to get something for us to drink. The hot sand burned my feet, and when I got back my father was up. He said he'd better go back and see how Mother was doing. Myra said she would go back with him because she already felt the blisters growing on her nose.

I told them I'd stay around the beach. My father gave me money. "In case you get hungry later," he said.

I walked back to the water and wondered if there was really any action under the boardwalk and if I should check it out. I walked along the water's edge and saw a crowd of kids watching some guys do gymnastics. I joined the group. It was a big surprise for me because I saw Lonesome Earl doing a balancing routine with one of the lifeguards. When he saw me he didn't stop what he was doing, but he said, "Hello, Gordie."

I could feel myself turning red under my sunburn because some of the kids looked at me. But I also felt kind of good that he did say hello. I stayed around and watched them go through some more routines, and when they had enough, Lonesome Earl came over to me.

"Whew, I'm out of shape," he said.

He looked in great shape to me with his muscles all shiny with sweat.

"How about a soda?" he said. Even though I just had one and I really wasn't thirsty for another, I said yes, because I felt sort of proud to be with Lonesome Earl. And I also figured it wouldn't hurt my cause in getting something from the dirty book store. I asked him how he got his muscles. I was kind of ashamed of my skinny body. He told me it came from hard work. He said he worked on a farm outside of Omaha, Nebraska, when he was younger. The idea of working on a farm really sounded great to me. I told him I'd never met anyone from Nebraska before.

"It wasn't all that great," he said. "I spent a lot of time in an orphanage, and then my foster parents had this farm. I sometimes think the only reason they took me in was to have an extra hand around the place. I'm not knocking it," he said, "because it sure beat the orphanage."

I followed him into the Texas Bar. When Dolores Monahan saw me she said in her tough way, "Go on, kid, take your piss someplace else."

"He's a friend of mine," said Lonesome Earl.

It made me real happy when he said that to her.

"Isn't he kind of young to be your pal?" she said, opening up two Cokes.

We went outside to drink them. It was just as well, because the Texas Bar smelled of stale beer and dirty feet. And also because Dolores Monahan made me feel kind of uncomfortable.

Lonesome Earl looked at me and I suddenly felt as if he was wondering about my crummy bathing suit.

"It belonged to my cousin," I said. "I'm going to get a new one."

"What?" he asked.

"This bathing suit. I hate it!" I said.

He laughed. "It's so unimportant. I really wouldn't have noticed if you hadn't brought it to my attention."

I had a feeling he was just trying to be nice.

"Gordie, you're going to be a real heartbreaker in no time at all," he said.

"Is that good or bad?" I said, really not knowing exactly what he meant.

He didn't answer right away. He took a swig from his Coke, and then he wiped his mouth with the back of his hand like I'd seen real cool guys do on TV.

"You're a good-looking kid, Gordie," he said. "And a heartbreaker is someone lots of people fall in love with."

"Then you must be a heartbreaker," I said.

He looked at me and rubbed my head. Tons of sand like a bad case of dandruff fell on my shoulders.

"Who knows, sandy-head?" he said. "Who knows?"

I wanted to bring up the subject of the dirty book store, but I just didn't know how. I just couldn't say, "How was the dirty book you got the other day?" and "Would you get one for me?" I just felt like the time wasn't right, but I sure wanted to ask him.

I thanked him for the soda and made up an excuse for leaving. I said that my family was expecting me back at the bungalow. I felt as if I'd made him uncomfortable, and as a result I was getting an uncomfortable feeling myself. I said, "So long."

He said, "Take care, now."

The thought of really going back to the bungalow came into my mind for about one second, but then I thought about facing another one of my mother's moods and quickly nixed that idea.

I thought about Lonesome Earl being brought up on a farm, and the idea didn't seem half so bad even though he was with foster parents. It was hard for me to understand why anyone would leave a farm for the city. Pictures of our dark airless apartment crossed my mind, and the bungalow was no better.

Walking past Amusement-O-Rama, I stopped in front of Gypsy Grandma. The hot spell really didn't do her any good because her face seemed to be drooping.

"You'd better watch out, Grandma," I said, "or you'll be ready for the candle factory soon."

Inside, the place was crowded with people off the beach—probably trying to get some relief from the sun. Some old people that I recognized from the Breeze Front were all dressed up, sitting and playing

Pokerino. The more I looked at them, the more I depressed myself. Like I realized this was a big thing for them.

I got change for Gypsy Grandma and said, "Sorry to make you work today!"

The fortune was the same as the one I got at the start of the summer. It said, "Someone out of the past will come back into your life." I figured old Grandma had run out of ideas, or else for sure now someone out of the past would really turn up.

I walked along the boardwalk, and the nearer I got to Luna Land, the more I thought about Fatty's Pizza Place and the action that was supposed to happen underneath it. But that was Larry's story and I didn't know if it was just baloney.

I got off of the boardwalk and decided to walk under it. It was a whole different scene. Like another world, shadowy and cool, with few people. Sometimes if I looked up through the spaces between the planks of the boardwalk I could see up someone's dress. But it wasn't any fun, because most of the time it was just an old person. It was a wild scene, with the people on the boardwalk making moving shadows beneath.

When I was just about under Fatty's Pizza Place I sat and rested my back against one of the wooden boardwalk piles. I sat there waiting for some action to take place, and just as I was getting real bored and ready to go, one of the tough girls from the Bath Beach section came under the boardwalk. And right after her came a lifeguard.

They acted real nervous, but they didn't see me. I saw them kiss and then I saw him grab her boobs. She didn't stop him either. After a while I heard him say he had to go back on duty.

She took a comb out from the bottom part of her bathing suit. I figured she had to be real easy, and I did something I'd never done before—maybe the courage came from Lonesome Earl telling me that I was going to be a heartbreaker. I just walked over to her and said, "Can I have a feel?"

She punched me in the mouth and yelled, "Get outta here, you little creep!"

As I ran away, I heard her yell, "Go home and play with yourself."

My lip hurt and I felt like crying. I ran into the ocean. The late afternoon sun was beginning to turn red. I pretended there was a great fire in the world and the only safe place was the ocean. I stayed in until my teeth began to chatter.

17

THE CURSE

"Gordie, Gordie!" At first it seemed like someone was calling my name in a dream, but when I opened my eyes Myra was standing over me.

"Gordie, something's wrong!" she sobbed quietly.

I sat up and rubbed my eyes with the palms of my hands. And then I looked at Myra and I knew right away what it was.

"There's something wrong with my face," she said. And when she spoke it was like when the dentist gives you a needle before pulling a tooth.

"I got up to go to the bathroom before, and I looked in the mirror." Myra began to sob real loud, and I knew she tried to cover it so she wouldn't wake my mother.

I felt all weak inside, and it just about ruined me to see Myra cry. I wanted to cry myself. Myra didn't have to finish her story. I could see there was something really wrong with her face.

"I can't close my eye, or move the right side of my mouth. It's like the whole side of my face is paralyzed," she said.

I wanted to say, "Rub it, and it will get better." But that was like something mother would have told us when we were little. Anyway, I knew this was more serious.

I couldn't really believe what had happened. But trying to make Myra feel better, and myself as well, I said, "Maybe it will go away in a little while—maybe you slept on it wrong."

Myra sat on the edge of my bed stroking the right side of her face. I thought about a cousin of ours who had died of polio when she was sixteen and we were little. I wondered if it was polio and if Myra thought the same thing.

I put my arm around Myra. She started to cry again, and the tears rolled down my face too.

"Oh, Gordie, what's going to happen? What shall we do?" Myra was suddenly a little girl again. And a memory from a long time ago came back to me.

Myra had broken a brand-new birthday doll, and

136

she sat on the edge of her bed and cried, and I remember sitting next to her and crying also. I wished I could have remained in that memory for a long time, but Myra's sobs broke through my thoughts.

"Does it hurt?" I asked her.

She shook her head no.

What had happened seemed like the kind of thing my mother would have told us about after speaking to my Aunt Sylvie on the phone. "Remember so-and-so?" she would say, and whether we remembered so-and-so or not, my mother would continue her story about some terrible thing that happened to them. But now it wasn't so-and-so, it was Myra.

Almost expecting some kind of trouble, my mother called from her room, "What's going on out there?"

And then Myra really let loose with crying.

My mother ran into the room in her nightgown. Her eyes looked wild. She looked at me and then at Myra. Her eyes opened wide and then she slapped both her cheeks and held her hands to her face and said nothing. She closed her eyes and rocked gently back and forth. Then she let her hands fall from her face, and opening her eyes, she looked upward and screamed, "Oh God, what are you doing to me?"

137

I got really scared. It was like my mother crossed over the line for sure, and she wasn't my mother anymore. "It happened!" she yelled. "We've been cursed!"

I really wondered if it was possible that I could have triggered this whole menopause thing and Myra's paralysis. The question of Widow Kravitz came back. I looked around the room and like I just wanted to vomit. I wondered if my mother secretly blamed me also.

I looked at Myra with her face strangely twisted, almost looking like Gypsy Grandma melting. And I was so scared that I couldn't cry. Instead I began to laugh. I don't know why I laughed, it just happened.

Myra looked at me and my mother came over to me and shouted, "What are you, an idiot?"

My mother's question made me laugh harder. She raised her hand to hit me, but I covered my face with my elbows outstretched. My mother put down her hand and slapped her thigh.

"Take me to a doctor," Myra cried. "Mama, please!"

I stopped laughing.

"Doctor?" shouted my mother. "We'll need a miracle!"

"I'm sorry, Myra, I only laughed because I was nervous."

"I know, Gordie," she said.

"I'm going to call Daddy," I said. "He'll know what to do."

My mother's hands were now in fistlike positions, and she walked around the room hitting the sides of her thighs.

"Mama, sit down," I said. "I'll take care of everything."

"You've taken care of everything!" she said.

She blamed me—I knew it. I got a terrible feeling and I wanted to run away. I was really sick to my stomach.

I got dressed in a hurry and I wondered if my father had arrived at work yet.

"Myra, get dressed!" my mother said with a strange kind of calm in her voice, as if suddenly she knew where the cure was.

When I left the bungalow most of the neighbors were looking from their windows or were on their porches. It was impossible for them not to have heard my mother.

"Gordie, is everything all right?" asked Mrs. Levenson.

"Is there something I can do, Gordie?" said Mrs. Friedman.

I shook my head no and started to cry. I ran all the way to Markey's. The store was just opening as I got there, and I beat Mr. Markey into his store as I ran to the phone.

When I called my father's place he hadn't arrived yet, and I told them the second he came in he should call me. I gave them Markey's number. I hung the phone up and sat in the booth. I shut my eyes and said, "Oh God, please make Myra all right again." The urge to throw up got even worse—the strong fish smell in the telephone booth didn't help. The phone, with all its dried fish blood and scales, really looked like it was dug up from the ocean, and as I looked at it, it rang. It scared me—it was like it had a life of its own.

"Hello, Daddy!" I said without even asking who it was.

"Gordie—?"

Before my father had a chance to say anything else, I began to cry again. "It's all my fault!"

"Gordie, what's the matter? Has something happened to Mother?" he asked.

"No, it's Myra," I said. Then I told him what happened.

"Gordie, don't cry," said my father. "It's not your fault. Just take Myra and Mother to Doctor Blaustein's, and I'll meet you there. Hurry, Gordie, and be careful."

Some of the neighbors were standing around the bungalow when I got back to it. Myra and my mother were already dressed. "Daddy said we should go to Doctor Blaustein's and he'd meet us there."

"Doesn't your father know that it's not a doctor we need?"

"Mother, let's hurry!" I said.

I reached for Myra's arm. "Come on, Myra," I said, and I sort of led her out of the bungalow. My mother followed us out, talking to herself and biting her lip and every once in a while gently slapping the side of her face.

Myra held her head down. "What's wrong?" said Mrs. Friedman, touching my mother's shoulder. My mother stopped and began to cry.

"Mother, come on!" I shouted. "Mrs. Friedman, tell Irwin I won't be in camp today."

"What's wrong?" she asked again. It seemed like my mother was about to tell her, but I went back and took my mother's arm. "Mother, please," I said. "We've got to hurry!"

Doctor Blaustein's office was in the city, and the

train ride back was a long one. My mother was like in a trance, and Myra kept looking down through most of the trip, and once in a while I could see her wiping a tear from her eye. "Do you think anyone can tell?" she whispered to me.

I found myself saying to her, "Don't worry, it's going to be all right."

The doctor's office was in a large apartment building that I had grown to hate because of the awful memories it brought back to me. I swallowed, and could still almost feel the terrible pain of the ear infection I once had.

My father was already there when we arrived, and he looked plenty worried. When he saw Myra, his eyes watered and turned red.

"We need a rabbi," said my mother. "It's a curse."

"Don't talk foolish," said my father.

My mother shook her head with a slight smile on her lips. She repeated the word, "Foolish."

My father and mother went into the doctor's office with Myra. And I was left alone in the waiting room. I wondered what was going through Myra's head, and in a way I wished it had happened to me instead of her.

The waiting room furniture was stiff and uncomfortable. There was a matched set of wooden chairs that looked like they belonged in a horror movie. Gnomelike faces were carved into the backs of them. One was grinning and one was frowning. I went over and pinched their noses. "Do you think it's my fault?" I said.

I tried to imagine what was going on in the doctor's office. I could almost see Doctor Blaustein, who was fat and bald with a scrubbed pink face, examining Myra with a little light. "Poor Myra," I said to myself.

The magazine table was stacked with lady-type magazines and medical ones too. I looked through the medical ones hoping to see some naked-people pictures but there weren't any. Just big color pictures of scabs, infections and burns. And lots of detailed drawings of veins and bones. No matter how hard I thought about it, I couldn't imagine all those things neatly tucked away in me. Liver and kidneys and intestines—I mean they just seemed like things that existed only in medical books and charts.

I came across an article on venereal disease that I began to read, but it was hard to concentrate on anything. I bit hard on my nails and just wished Myra would walk out of the doctor's office smiling and saying something like, "It happened because I slept on the wrong side, and see—it's all better now!"

The office door opened and Myra came out looking just as scared as when she went in. My mother and father remained in the doctor's office, and I wondered if they were talking about my mother's menopause.

"Well, what is it?" I asked Myra.

"I forget—it has a funny name," she said.

"Will it go away?" I asked.

"I hope so," she said. "He said it will."

The office door opened again and my father came out, leaving my mother in there alone with the doctor.

"Everything's going to be all right, isn't it?" I said.

"In time," said my father. "With Myra and Mother."

"What's Myra's thing called?"

"It's called Bell's palsy," he said. "It has to do with the seventh cranial nerve, which controls the facial muscles." My father sounded like some doctor. Then he looked at Myra and he forced a cheeriness to his voice. "Fortunately, eighty percent recover within a few weeks."

"I have to come here for electric diathermy treatments," said Myra. The right side of her mouth sagged, and saliva trickled onto her face.

My bottom lip quivered, and I tried hard not to cry.

"Oh, well, what's a few weeks?" I said, hoping in some way to make things a little easier for Myra.

"And Mother is going to be visiting the doctor also," said my father. "She's going to be getting treatments."

"What kind of treatments?" I asked.

"Hormone shots," whispered Myra.

My mother came out of the doctor's office wiping a tear from her eye.

"Thank you, Doctor," said my father. Doctor Blaustein walked into the waiting room and came over to me.

"How do you feel, Gordie?" he asked.

I told him I was just fine. Even if I really had some awful sickness, right then I wouldn't have told him.

"He's getting to be quite a man," the doctor said, putting his hand on the back of my neck.

My father told me to take good care of Myra and my mother. And he said to Myra, "You'll see—in no time at all it's going to be fine."

Myra tried to smile, and the crooked expression on her face brought a whole new round of tears into my eyes.

On the train ride back, my mother kept saying, "We've been cursed, we've been cursed!"

I couldn't get rid of my lousy feeling, and my mother's talk made me feel even worse. I couldn't wait until the hormone shots began to work.

18

THE SECRET VISIT

No matter how hard I tried, I still couldn't erase from my mind the possibility that I might have had something to do with all this. In spite of my mother's changes, she was still right a lot of times about her feelings when things were going to happen. There was proof of those. So, much as I thought about it, I still couldn't rule out the idea of a Kravitz curse. It was possible that Mr. Steiner had lied to my mother. My mother could always tell when I lied to her.

My father and mother had a big argument as to whether we'd finish the summer out at the beach. My mother kept insisting that we go. And when I said I thought we should go too, my father said,

147

"You stay out of this, Gordie." And he added, "Did you forget about your job?"

My father also said that in my mother's present state of mind she wasn't capable of making the best decisions.

"It will be good for Myra to be in the sun and the fresh air. In the city she'd just be cooped up in the apartment."

I told Myra that I wouldn't go to camp anymore, and that I would stay home until she got better.

"Thanks, Gordie," she said. "But there are a lot of kids depending on you."

"Oh, screw the kids and the puppets," I said, and I meant it. It all seemed far away and unimportant.

"Gordie, what kind of talk is that? You've made a commitment and now you have the responsibility of carrying it out."

Commitment, responsibility—they were winter words that seemed to belong locked in some school supply closet.

"Gordie, for me," she said.

I was silent for a while, "Okay, for you," I said.

"And it's going to be brilliant?" she asked. I knew she was trying hard to make me feel good.

"It'll be brilliant, and I'll dedicate it to you."

Now I knew I was going out of my way to make Myra feel good. But I never really know how to act when someone is sick. I suppose I should just act regular, but I felt that I had to show Myra something extra special. I mean she *is* the only sister I have.

At camp everyone asked me how Myra was. Arlene said, "I thought strokes only happen to older people."

I didn't feel like telling her what Myra really had, but it's kind of wild how all kinds of crazy rumors spread. I told her that Myra was really eighty-five years old. Irwin asked me if it would be all right for him to see Myra. I could only shrug my shoulders and say, "It's up to her."

Stanley Morgan came over to me and said how sorry he was to hear about Myra, and if I had to spend time with her he would understand. "Feel free to come and go as you please," he said.

I knew he meant it. And I thanked him and said, "We're going to have a great puppet show and carnival."

"Boy, is that a relief," he said. "You know, Gordie, I don't know what we'd do without you."

I got a good feeling. It was better than if someone had told me I'd just won something. It was the first time anyone had ever really counted on me.

As I sorted out the puppet pieces, I still couldn't help but wonder who had done them in.

Myra wouldn't see Irwin—as a matter of fact Myra wouldn't see anyone. She just read, watched TV or played solitaire. She wouldn't move from the bungalow except when she and my mother went to the doctor's for treatment.

One day after treatment my mother said, "She's not getting better. A doctor can't help her." She spoke as if Myra wasn't there. Myra ran into her room and cried.

I ran after Myra. "Mother doesn't know what she's talking about," I said. "It's those changes of hers. You know she's just not herself."

"Look at me, Gordie. Nothing's happening. Maybe she's right. Do you think Steiner lied to mother about the Widow Kravitz?" said Myra.

Myra said what I had been thinking, but I was afraid to come out and say it. I just looked at Myra, unable to give her any kind of answer, because I didn't know anything for sure.

I heard a cat crying again outside of the bungalow. "Hey, maybe it's the same silly cat," I said. I thought if I brought it in, it would cheer Myra up a little.

"Don't go near it, Gordie!" she cried.

At night when I was in bed I heard the cat again,

only it sounded like it was on the porch. I thought I saw a shadow pass the window. I put the pillow over my head. I thought about the lemony tea smell on Myra's robe after she held the cat, and I felt cold all over.

The next day when I got home from camp, my mother greeted me all excited. I thought maybe Myra's face was all better, but it wasn't. "I've been doing some investigating," said my mother. "There is this rabbi who heads up a congregation in a synagogue in the neighborhood I was raised in, and he knows how to deal with things of this nature."

"What can a rabbi do?" I asked.

"Now is not the time for questions," said my mother. "It's just important that we get to him as soon as possible!"

"Does he have some kind of special medicine?" I asked.

"His kind of medicine you don't get from doctors or drugstores," said my mother.

I knew my mother was talking about some kind of hocus-pocus, and the whole thing seemed so insane in a way, but my mother was determined. And Myra seemed so helpless and almost willing to go along with anything. In a way, I couldn't blame her.

Mother made me and Myra swear that we

wouldn't breathe a word of this to Father. The synagogue was in a decaying part of the city. Most of the stores were boarded up and the buildings were abandoned. We passed a movie theater that advertised dirty movies. "To think I used to come here as a girl," said my mother. It was hard to imagine my mother as ever having been a girl—it seemed like something that must have taken place in another lifetime. Her hair was very gray and uncombed and her face looked haggard. My father once said when he first saw her, he thought she was one of the prettiest girls he had ever seen.

The synagogue had once been a barbershop, and the barber pole still stood in front of it. A Star of David almost as badly painted as the ones on Larry's sneakers was on the window. Underneath were the words HOUSE OF SOLOMON CONG.

How my mother ever heard about this place was a mystery to Myra and me, but to hear my mother talk it was like we were going to visit some miracle man.

Suddenly Myra was frightened. She tugged at Mother's arm. "Let's go," she said. "This is all so crazy. Doctor Blaustein will help me—you'll see."

I could tell Myra was really shook, and I was pretty nervous about this whole thing myself. I mean,

152

what was this rabbi going to do that some other rabbi couldn't?

Mother pretended not to hear Myra and she knocked on the glass door with her ring. "He's probably at the beach," I said. "Let's go!"

Making a visor with her hands over her brows, Mother pressed her face close to the glass.

"Good, he's coming," she said. "Now remember, not a word of this to your father."

I really hated the whole idea of this thing, especially the part about not telling my father, and Myra felt the same way. But my mother seemed so desperate.

The man who opened the door introduced himself as Rabbi Kraunwald.

"I'm Mrs. Cassman," said my mother, stepping inside the store synagogue and sort of pushing Myra in. "This is my daughter, the one I told you about on the phone."

She didn't even bother to introduce me, but I followed them in. I was surprised she didn't point to me and say, "That's the one who started the whole thing."

Rabbi Kraunwald was an old clean-shaven man with a double wart on the side of his face that possibly with any more size to it would be the start of another head. I knew all about how it wasn't polite to stare, but this wart was really something. I couldn't imagine what good the rabbi could do for Myra if he couldn't get rid of that thing on his face —or else maybe that was part of his magic.

The barber mirrors were still up, giving the place a feeling of being larger than it was. There were rows of benches, and what might have been the world's smallest altar. If it had been any smaller it could've fit inside Harold's dollhouse.

Myra and I sat on a back bench and I knotted my handkerchief at the corners, making a yarmulke for myself.

My mother and the rabbi whispered to each other, stopping every once in a while to look at us. The rabbi came over to Myra and asked her if she believed in God. Myra shook her head yes. Then he and my mother talked some more. My mother reached into her pocketbook and took out a roll of money and handed it to the rabbi, who stuffed it into his jacket pocket without even counting it. My mother seemed very satisfied with herself.

"Now everything is going to be all right," she said, sort of talking to herself.

"What's it all about?" I asked her.

"You'll know in time," said my mother.

The sun wasn't out but it was really hot and humid. My mother suggested that we go for a soda. Myra wanted to go right back, but my mother said it would be good for her. It was hard to find a place to get a soda in that neighborhood, and when we finally did, it wasn't worth the search because the guy didn't know how to make a good ice cream soda. I hardly touched mine, not because it wasn't good, but because it really upset me to see Myra tackle hers. If any liquid or food got into the right side of her mouth it would kind of slip out. She kept bringing a napkin up to her mouth and trying to make some joke about it. But I knew that was just for my benefit.

When mother asked me why I wasn't finishing my soda I told her it tasted lousy. On the train trip back, Myra and I tried to guess what mother's secret conference and payoff were all about. We could only figure it had to do with religion and praying. And we tried to guess how mother ever found out about that synagogue in the first place.

Back at the bungalow I tried to get Myra to go to the beach with me, but she wouldn't.

Myra continued going to Doctor Blaustein for therapy. And my mother made another visit to the rabbi by herself.

Myra's face didn't show any noticeable change. And when Irwin came by she wouldn't see him—or anyone else. She even stopped writing in her diary. One night Irwin brought a big stuffed panda, but that didn't coax her out, and he left it in the rocking chair on the porch.

I began to think of elaborate plans to get Myra out and doing things, but everything seemed to fizzle. I told her that I needed her help at camp with the show, and that she was the only person in the whole world that could help me. But that didn't work.

I even suggested that we go hunting for seashells, but she said, "Gordie, it won't work, I just want to be left alone."

It really depressed the hell out of me. And as if things weren't bad enough, my mother and father began to argue about money. It was something they had never done before.

I wondered what my father would do if I told him about Rabbi Kraunwald and the barbershop synagogue.

19

HEARTBREAKER CHILD

My mother made several more trips to her old neighborhood and the rabbi. Neither Myra or I could pry anything out of her. Neighbors came by with different remedies, claiming they either knew someone that had the very same thing, or else they had heard about it from someone. Their remedies included everything from drinking carrot juice twelve times a day to taking hot vinegar baths.

Although it was kind of hard for me to swallow, since I felt at fault, I was beginning to think that maybe the whole theory of there being a curse was completely true. Especially since Doctor Blaustein's electrotherapy didn't seem to be having much effect. The hormone shots might have calmed my mother down, but it didn't help her depressed condition, which seemed to be getting worse.

The whole thing was getting to me. It just killed me to see Myra and my mother the way they were. My interest in the show was zero. I tried hard to hide my feelings so the kids wouldn't catch on. It was important to them. Avram really helped me with the puppets. He worked extra hard, and it wasn't too long before they began to take shape again. I sort of had thoughts about Avram knocking himself out on the puppets because of a possible guilt feeling. But when I looked at him real hard I just couldn't get myself to believe that he could be the culprit.

Stanley Morgan pitched in and helped make the stage, which was really going to be terrific—with two sets of curtains, one that opened and closed and one that went up and down. He really knew a lot about stages, because he put in an elaborate set of lights. His enthusiasm began to rub off on me a little, and my interest began to pick up.

I'd report what was happening to Myra, hoping that she'd want to see it all for herself, but she'd only say, "That sounds nice."

When the Anna puppet was all costumed and strung up, I took her home to show Myra, but when I got there she still hadn't returned from the doctor.

I felt a big letdown, and the bungalow was especially gloomy. Then it happened. All at once I was hit with a feeling like I wanted to die. I sat on the porch and toyed with the puppet. The sky was yellow-gray, like the color of smoke you can get from a chemistry set. Everything felt sticky and there was almost like an acid in the air that made my eyes burn. I had to get away from the bungalow. I put the puppet away and walked toward the boardwalk. Ever since the puppet massacre and Myra's face thing, I'd been purposely avoiding Larry. I was sort of chicken about facing up to him and maybe his connection with it. I'd even thought that maybe he'd had Harold do it for him. Sort of like the mad doctor who laughed in the shadows while his hunchbacked assistant robbed some grave.

The beach was empty except for some kids necking under blankets. I envied them. I'd thought for sure I would have had a girl friend this summer. There were times I almost felt like calling Phyllis Lavine, the girl I knew from school. I thought it would have been nice to invite her down to the beach, but not the way my mother had been acting.

A lot of the concession people stood around and gloomily looked out from their stands. I guess they figured it was going to be a rainy, no-business night.

I walked along the boardwalk and felt as if I didn't belong to anything or anyone. It was a funny kind of feeling, like there was a big thick piece of glass separating me from the rest of the world. I walked past the Texas Bar hoping I would run into Lonesome Earl. The idea of him getting me a dirty book didn't seem so important although I wouldn't have minded one. It's just that I wanted to see him, and hoped that maybe he'd talk to me again.

The bar was filled with people who had already had too much to drink, and they were loud. The janitor from the Breeze Front was having an argument with some guy. The janitor kept saying, "In your hat, in your hat!" I hated to see people drunk. It was like they had no control, and I felt embarrassed for them.

The gray clouds over the ocean darkened, and it made me think of war and frightened people, and then I was back to Myra.

"Whatcha thinkin' about?" I really jumped, but I smiled when I saw it was Lonesome Earl. "If I scared you, I'm sorry," he said. "You looked like you were really thinking up a storm."

"That would be kind of wild, to think up a storm," I said.

"It looks like we just might have one," he said.

"But I won't tell anyone who was responsible for it."

I laughed. Then I told him about what I had been thinking about and when I got to the Myra part, I had to wipe some tears away from my face. I really felt like a first class stupid jerk for letting him see me cry. For some reason he was the one person on earth that I didn't want to see me cry. I mean I didn't want to give him the impression that I was just a dumb kid. Then I began to make all kinds of apologies. And he said, "Hey, cut it out."

Just my luck, I had to blow my nose real bad and I didn't have a handkerchief. He took out a neatly folded red-and-white one and handed it to me. I was really too ashamed to take it, but suddenly it was an emergency. The handkerchief smelled good.

I thanked him, and when I wanted to give him his handkerchief back, he told me to keep it. I told him I was glad he saw me, and how I was looking for him and what kind of mood I was in. He looked at me for a minute, and it seemed to me by the expression on his face that he was moved by what I had said.

He must have sensed my knowing this, and he broke the mood by faking a laugh and pointing to the kids rolling around under the blankets on the beach.

"It looks like they're having a ball. Do you have a girl?" he asked. I shook my head no, and wanted to ask him the same question, but I didn't.

A strong wind blew from the beach and the necking kids hollered and laughed, and I could taste sand in my mouth. We walked toward Luna Land, and when we passed the dirty book store, I had a strong urge to ask him if he'd get me a dirty book, but all I said was, "That store wasn't there last year."

He completely ignored what I said, and just didn't pick up on it. I felt as if I'd let a good chance go by. Sand blew across the boardwalk and it almost hurt. Lonesome Earl walked on the ocean side and tried to act as a shield.

"It reminds me of the hailstorms on the farm," he said. He began to talk about his childhood in the orphanage and his foster family.

Then I began to tell him about my family and about Myra, and I found myself telling him about how my mother thinks it's a curse.

"Are you afraid of things like curses?" I asked.

"No, Gordie," he said. Then he thought awhile and continued talking. "It's the real things I'm afraid of."

It wasn't hard to tell that he must have been re-membering things.

Then he said, "When I was in the orphanage and I was bad, they shaved my head—and other things . . ." his voice dropped.

"I never knew anyone that had been in an orphan-age," I said. An orphanage seemed like something that existed in books written long ago. And to hear Lonesome Earl talk about it, it became a very real thing. And I began to feel good about having a family. I just wished things would go back the way they were before. Like Myra's face would be per-fect again and my mother's changes would have stopped.

"When things are better," I said, "you can come and have dinner with us."

"Thanks," he said. "Hey, I hope you're not feelin' sorry for me."

"No," I said, but I was.

"Someday I'm going to be rich and famous. I have an audition coming up for a club date in the city," he said. "I even write my own songs."

He began to sing a song that he told me he had just finished. "You're in this song, Gordie," he said, "listen." And when he came to a line about a heartbreaker child with a warm summer smile, he said, "That's you, Gordie."

"You're kidding," I said. "You just made it up."

"No, Gordie, I'm not kidding. I didn't just make it up and it is you."

I suddenly got an almost scared kind of feeling. But in a way it was mixed with excitement. Like I felt important.

"Hey, how about a hot dog?" he asked, going over to the stand. I looked up at the clock above it and figured that my mother and Myra had to be back by now.

"No thanks, I've got to go back," I said. I ran off the boardwalk feeling better than I had before. But then I suddenly felt kind of crummy, because I had forgotten to wish Lonesome Earl good luck with his city audition.

My mother and Myra still hadn't returned from the doctor's, and I began to wonder where they were. Sitting alone in the bungalow, I was beginning to have some regrets about not asking Lonesome Earl to get me a dirty book.

I picked up the Anna puppet and made her dance on the table.

20

THE BLACKOUT

My mother and Myra both came into the bungalow crying. When I asked Myra why they were late and what was the matter, she ran into her room saying, "I'll tell you later."

Drying her eyes and putting an apron on, my mother sort of had control of herself and said, "You'll have to settle for a hurry-up supper tonight."

I told her that I was so hungry I could eat a wart omelette. I was sorry I said it, because it set off a whole new flood of tears for Myra and hysterical crying for my mother. She ran into her room and said I'd have to make my own supper. I thought about what I had said, and I couldn't believe it could have triggered off the scene that it did.

I made myself a cranberry omelette and I asked Myra if she wanted any. She said that she wasn't hungry. While I ate, I tried to figure out why Rabbi Kraunwald's warts would set my mother off again. It was really bugging me. It began to rain, and the screen door blew open from the wind. My mother and Myra came out of their rooms.

"If I don't get a heart attack it will be a miracle," said my mother.

The lights in the bungalow began to flicker. "Quick, Gordie, get the candles." I must give my mother credit for always being prepared. She had plenty of candles stashed away in case of emergency. And it looked like one was about to happen. The lights dimmed once again, and then they went out completely. I wondered if Myra was afraid, and I made some bright comment like, "To think this is how they lived in olden days."

"In olden days they were used to it," said Myra. We all sat around the table with candles in every imaginable container—glasses, bottles, plates.

"It's a perfect night for a séance," I said. My mother gave me a dirty look. Then she focused her attention on a low white candle. "I remember when I was a girl I used to look forward to Friday night to see my mother light the Sabbath candles. I thought it was such a beautiful custom. I used to do it when I first got married, but then I stopped." My mother stopped talking and sighed. Then she continued, "Things were so different then."

It seemed like remembering the past changed my mother's mood. Myra began to talk about my grandmother, and other things from the past. "I remember Passover at Grandma's, and, Mother, remember how you dressed up as Elijah the prophet, and knocked on the back door and scared us?"

Then I said, "Remember how last summer we were afraid of Mr. Green, the carpenter at Stutman's? He'd go to the butcher and fill his shopping cart with gizzards and chicken hearts, and we always thought he was some kind of evil man."

"Until we found out that he just had a soft spot for cats, and he had nine million of them," said Myra.

"Do you know," I said, "when you think about it, all the scary things we sort of made up ourselves."

Sitting around the table with just the candles there was a closeness and a quiet that I hadn't felt in a long time. My mother's attention was on a sputtering flame, and when she did look up toward the door she screamed. I felt the hairs on the back of my neck bristle, and Myra froze.

I heard someone running off of the porch. "There was something strange at the door," said my mother. Her hands were outstretched over her heart and her voice sounded dry.

As I got up to run to the porch, Myra said, "Gordie, don't go!" But I did, and I couldn't see anything. I was glad because I was plenty scared.

When my father came home, my mother said, "Thank God!" Then she told him what had happened.

"Maybe it was someone who came to visit, and you scared them off," said my father.

"Gordie, Gordie," said an eerie voice. I went to the porch. It was Larry, with a big black umbrella and a flashlight.

"Isn't this blackout great?" he said.

I didn't answer his question, but I asked him one instead. "Were you here a little while ago?"

"Me? No!" he said.

Larry was a good liar, and I had my suspicions, but as usual no proof.

"Haven't seen you in a while," I said.

"I was just going to say the same thing to you," he said.

I knew why I was avoiding Larry, but I realized that Larry must have also been avoiding me. I wondered why.

There was loud screaming coming from the Breeze Front and then we heard fire engines. Larry and I ran over there, and at first all I could see was smoke pouring out from one of the top windows, and then I saw the flames.

Everyone crowded into the street, and the firemen kept telling everyone to stay back. An old man was stranded on the top porch, and it seemed to take forever for the ladder to get to him. I crossed all my fingers, and when the firemen finally reached him I just about cried.

"Too bad!" said Larry. "If he had died by fire, when he reached the other world he would have been in charge of the League of Forty Demons."

"What do you have to die by to be in charge of the Fifty-Demon League?" I said.

Larry ignored my remark. "You might as well say good-bye to the Breeze Front," he said.

And he was right. The old place was going fast, and the whole top part was in flames and looked like a giant torch lighting up the whole street, sending sparks flying off in all directions.

The man the firemen had rescued was the caretaker, and I wondered if he had started it in one of his alcoholic moods.

"Steiner's might be next," said Larry.

Terrible images of my family trapped in the burning bungalow went through my head. I raced back there and the lights still weren't on. My mother and father watched the fire from the porch.

I went into the bungalow and Myra was still sitting at the table. "You should see the fire—it really is something, sparks are flying everywhere. I mean like even this bungalow is in danger."

"Couldn't think of a better fate for it," said Myra.

I remembered that Myra had said she would tell me about why she and my mother were late getting back that day, and what the crying was about.

But the lights went back on and my mother and father came back into the bungalow.

"Those poor people at the Breeze Front," said my father. "Their summer is ruined."

"*Their* summer is ruined?" said my mother.

21

THE REHEARSAL

By the time the first morning light came through the windows, the bungalow smelled like a potato you make over an open fire. And it seemed as if the bungalow had a smoke cloud hovering over it. I thought about how the Breeze Front had sort of lived for so many years, and then how something like a fire could destroy it all so fast. I thought about the puppets also, and how long and how much work went into making them, and when they had been destroyed, it took like no time at all. I wondered if the Breeze Front could ever take shape again like the puppets did.

I dressed in a hurry because I wanted to get to

camp early. Today was going to be the first complete rehearsal of the show.

When I came out of the bathroom, Myra was sitting at the table. Her chin rested in her hands, so that part of her mouth was hidden, and for a second her face looked all right again. But then she dropped her hands into her lap, and it was easy to see nothing had changed.

I could tell she had her own gray cloud around her. And I tried to think of something nice and encouraging to say but I couldn't. I couldn't think of anything funny either. I said something dumb about the fire, and I don't even think she heard me.

Myra broke her silence with a laugh-cry kind of sound. It surprised me, and I was about to ask her what she was thinking when she began to talk.

"Oh Gordie, it's all so stupid!" she said. And the word "stupid" seemed to twist her mouth even more. "You know that rabbi—well, he's not a rabbi, he's a phony!"

"I knew there was something strange about that barbershop synagogue," I said.

"We went to him straight from the doctor, and the place was closed down! There were boards across the window. You should have been there, Gordie—I thought Mother was going to smash some-

172

thing through the door. Do you know that he told Mother he was going to make a health-restoring gold crown for me, and that he was going to have ten holy men pray for me for thirty consecutive days."

I began to laugh, and then I told Myra I was sorry. "That might be one of the dumbest things I've ever heard," I said.

"It really isn't any laughing matter. It cost Mother a lot of money."

"Where did she hear about him in the first place?"

"I think she told me from Aunt Sylvie's dressmaker."

"It figures," I said. "Do you remember how she used to threaten Cousin Lowell when he wouldn't eat? I found out from Lowell himself. She used to tell him that if he didn't eat he'd get skinny and ugly like me. I never forgave her for that; now this is something else to hate her for."

Myra smiled. "And look at Lowell now, he's such a creep. And you're beautiful, Gordie, you really are."

I went over to Myra and I hugged her and said, "Boy, am I glad you're my sister."

She kissed me on my cheek and I hugged her tighter. I could feel her tears rolling down my face.

"I'm not going through what you are, Myra, so

I'm not really in a position to talk, but I know everything is going to work out. And I'm sure Doctor Blaustein is going to help you. He's always helped me."

"Gordie, you used to be so little, now you're bigger than me," said Myra standing up.

When I got onto the porch, I turned and pushed my face against the screen door. "You'll see, Myra, Mother is going to be okay too," I whispered.

I wanted so hard to believe what I had said.

At camp everyone was excited about the first rehearsal. Avram got the part of Anna's son, and Dee Dee got the part of the King's girl friend. They both seemed happy about it.

First rehearsal was a complete disaster. And I really got into a deep funk thinking that the whole thing was probably one big mistake. Like the whole summer. Stanley Morgan tried to cheer me up, and said, "What can you expect from a first rehearsal?"

When I went home from camp that day, there were posters along the boardwalk advertising the camp carnival and puppet show. I had strange, mixed feelings when I saw them. It was exciting seeing something I had worked on being advertised for everyone to come and look at. But the way things had gone that day, I also got a scared feeling.

Back at the bungalow, things were in reverse. Myra was trying to cheer *me* up. "Don't worry, it's going to be a great show. I have confidence in you, Gordie," she said.

I asked her if she was going to be there, and she answered with, "We'll see."

I wanted Myra to be there so much.

The next few days at camp things really began to improve. And I was getting the feeling of what it might be like to hit a home run with bases loaded, tie score, at the end of the ninth inning. I mean everyone was all over me in a good way.

It was raining when I left the camp one afternoon. I ran along the boardwalk and felt my clothes begin to stick to me. I could see my skin through my shirt. I stopped running and went by the Texas Bar to get my breath and shake myself out. Lonesome Earl was sitting at the bar. He had a drink in front of him and I could tell that he must have had a few more before that one.

"Gordie!" he shouted. "If you were old enough I'd buy you a drink."

I suddenly felt funny seeing him that way.

"Dolores, get the gentleman a Coke," he said. "I'm celebrating, Gordie. I got the job at the club in the city."

"That's great," I said. I raised my Coke like it was a toast and then I said, "Congratulations!"

"Bottoms up!" he said, picking up his drink. "Here's to you, Gordie." He winked, and gulped it down.

He pulled the ring from the scarf he was wearing around his neck and dropped the scarf onto my head.

"Dry your head," he said.

"It'll get ruined," I said, handing it back to him.

"There's more where that came from," he said, putting the scarf back on my head and rubbing it. "I'm going to make a lot of money, Gordie."

"When you're rich and famous will you remember me?" I asked.

He looked at me, first seriously, then breaking into a smile. "Gordie, I'll always remember you."

I could tell the drinks were really going right to his head, because his eyes looked all watery.

The next day the posters along the boardwalk hung kind of limp, and it was hard to tell what they were about. I walked to the camp running a stick I'd found along the top of the boardwalk railing.

"Hey, Gordie," Larry called from the beach.

I hung over the boardwalk railing. "Whatcha doing out so early?" I asked.

"I thought I'd go crabbing," he said. "Do you want to come?"

I told him I was on my way to work.

"I saw the posters," he said. "You're going to have to do them over."

"So we'll do them over!"

"I heard you had to do the dolls over too," he laughed.

I figured that was it—Larry showing his hand—and now it was up to me to think of some kind of revenge.

I broke the stick I was carrying in half. "See you later," I said, throwing the pieces off of the boardwalk onto the sand, barely missing Larry.

22

REVENGE

If Doctor Blaustein was helping my mother, it was kind of hard to tell, because Myra's thing really had her going. And even before the changes began, if one of us got sick my mother really worried.

And if the bungalow was still giving off bad vibrations, that too was hard to tell. It was sort of like when I once went to a play, and for about the first few minutes I was looking at the stage setting, but once things started happening I didn't even notice the set anymore. It became a part of what was happening—I mean you couldn't separate it. Well anyway, that's how it was with the bungalow.

My revenge plans for Larry narrowed down to giving him a good case of the runs by feeding him a chocolate laxative and hoping he'd think it was candy.

I set up a crabbing date with him and figured then I would give him his medicine. I sort of got some kind of crazy enjoyment just thinking about it. When the morning came I tried to be real cool about it. I even packed a bag of fruit, cookies and the chocolate revenge. I was so eager to get started that I even went to his bungalow to get him.

It was a clear, sunny Saturday and although the crabs weren't biting, Larry was. I mean like he was even greedy about the chocolate. I had to hold myself back from just coming out and laughing and maybe ruining the whole thing.

I got a little scared when Larry asked me why I was in such a good mood. I told him I was just happy to have a day off. When we got tired of crabbing we stretched out on the sand. I watched a skywriting plane at work. I thought it would be great if he could write out some message like, "Larry Perl is going to have a case of the runs."

I knew this was the only way to do it, because if I punched Larry in the nose and accused him of his foul deed he'd just pretend to be all hurt and deny it. Or else he'd punch me back, and he's bigger.

He told me that Luna Land was having a half-price day and he had promised to take Harold. "It'll be a lot of laughs," he said. I told him that I thought it sounded like fun, and I agreed to meet him later that day in front of Luna Land.

I went to the camp and did some final touch-up work on the puppets. For the first time I was able to sit back and just look at them, and they really seemed kind of good. Myra's idea for *The King and I* was really a great one, and I had told her so. I really had hoped she would break down and say yes, and come to see the show. Even my mother and father said they would come to see it.

I arrived early for my meeting with Larry and Harold. Because of the special prices that day the place was really packing them in. I saw the girl from under the boardwalk, and I tried to hide by looking in a funny mirror with a bunch of nuns.

I began to wonder if the chocolate laxative had begun to work and if Larry was going to be late or show at all. But when he arrived with Harold I figured nothing had happened yet. Harold walked kind of funny now that his casts were off, and I couldn't help but feel sorry for him.

We bought our tickets and went in. "We're going to have a good time, aren't we?" Larry said to Harold. Harold shook his head yes. I couldn't tell if

Larry was being sincere or if this whole thing was a big put-on, and in some way Larry was going to get his kicks.

I had a feeling it was to get his kicks, because Larry winked at me. "Hey, maybe Harold shouldn't go on the rides," I said, really worried that something might happen to him.

"Well, if he gets killed on the roller coaster, in the other world he can be in charge of a League of a Thousand Demons! Isn't that right, Harold?"

Harold just smiled and shook his head. I wondered how far Larry could really go. The first ride we went on was the Tilt-a-Whirl, and the three of us sat together, with Harold in between. When the ride really got going, it was hard for me to tell if Harold was enjoying himself. He just drooled a lot, some of it getting on my shirt. The carousel was the next ride, but I stayed off of it. Larry sat on a stationary horse while Harold rode the kind that went up and down. He really seemed to get a charge out of that one. Larry would sort of goose him every time his horse came down.

"Come on, let's go on the roller coaster now," said Larry. "Enough of this baby crap."

"Hey, Larry, do you think it's a mistake?" I asked, nodding toward Harold.

181

"You're like an old worrywart." He laughed. "Come on, don't be an old fart!" he said, running on line to get the tickets.

I sat alone in one car and Larry and Harold sat together in back of me. Luna Land had a really terrific roller coaster—it really scared the hell out of me, and in a way I was chicken about going on. But I knew what I would have to put up with if I refused to go.

Anyway, just as the thing got started I turned around to look at Harold and Larry. And from the expression on Larry's face, it wasn't hard to tell that my chocolate revenge was beginning. I let out with probably the greatest wolf calls of all time. When the ride came to an end, Larry ran off and left me standing with Harold.

"Larry is such a nice boy," I said to Harold.

Harold shook his head yes.

I got stuck with the job of taking Harold back home, but it was worth it. I bought him a banana frozen custard that he attacked like he'd never seen food before. I walked along the boardwalk laughing to myself. Larry's expression was one that I knew I would never forget as long as I lived.

"I don't think Larry feels too well," I said. Talking to Harold was practically like talking to yourself. "He isn't the only one who can play at that stupid demon game!" I laughed some more.

When I passed Amusement-O-Rama, I sort of looked in. It was just something I did out of habit, and then I did a double take. At first I thought I was seeing a ghost, but when I looked real hard I saw that it was Widow Kravitz, sitting and playing Pokerino. I ran the rest of the way to the bungalow, almost dragging Harold along. I left him out on the porch when I ran inside.

"She's alive!" I shouted. "I just saw Widow Kravitz playing Pokerino."

"On Saturday, never!" said my mother. "You're lying."

"I'm not! I'm not! Believe me!" I said. "Myra, you believe me. Please come with me, I'll show her to you."

"It's hard to believe," said Myra.

"I wouldn't lie to you, Myra," I said. "Come with me, please." I wish I could have said, "Tell them, Harold, you saw her also." Harold just stood on the porch looking through the screen door.

"This isn't a trick of yours to get me out on the boardwalk, is it?" asked Myra.

"No, Myra, come before it's too late and she's gone. I swear to you it's no trick."

"Okay, I'll get ready. You don't expect me to go out looking like this," she said, touching her hair and her robe.

I told her I was taking Harold back, and when I returned to be ready.

When I got back my mother kept saying, "It's impossible. You were mistaken, Gordie, today is Saturday."

"Come too," I pleaded with my mother.

I ran there with Myra, taking a shortcut now that the Breeze Front was out of business. We were able to run freely along the back path of the Breeze Front that went directly to the boardwalk. Before, if I tried to go that way, someone would always yell that I was trespassing.

When we got to Amusement-O-Rama, she was gone. Myra's face first looked disappointed, and then she seemed angry. "It was all a trick! Wasn't it?"

"No!" I practically cried. "She really was here."

"It's hard to believe, Gordie."

"Maybe if we look along the boardwalk?" I said.

"In this crowd?" said Myra.

"You're already on the boardwalk," I said. "Let's look."

Myra and I looked at every old lady up and down

the boardwalk. But there wasn't a sign of Widow Kravitz.

I really felt let down and I looked at Myra like I wanted to cry. She looked at me and shook her head, like a mother does when her child does something naughty.

"Since we're here, let's have a frozen custard," she said. "I've been dying for one."

We walked slowly back to the bungalow and I said it wasn't a trick and how now that she was on the boardwalk with all those people and no one looked at her strangely, it would be a good idea if she went out all the time.

"My big little brother is so full of advice," she said.

You could have knocked us over with a piece of paper when we got back to the bungalow. Widow Kravitz was sitting with my mother and having a cup of tea.

"Mrs. Kravitz is here to pick up her hat," my mother said.

She said she would have come sooner, but she had been away on a trip. She told my mother that she was tired of bungalows.

"So are we," said my mother, laughing. "I think next year we'll take a trip."

I suddenly realized that my mother had laughed for the first time all summer. And whether it was Dr. Blaustein's hormone shots or Widow Kravitz's visit, it just didn't matter. I was happy to see her smile.

Myra smiled too and I wished it wasn't a crooked one.

23

CHINESE LANTERNS AND PAPER CUPS

I felt like a sticky wet lollypop in a woolen blanket while I worked the puppets. It wasn't the most comfortable feeling in the world, but it was worth it. We had sold lots of tickets, and it seemed like everyone was really eating up the show. What really made me especially happy was my mother and father being there with Myra.

The show went great except on Anna's final bow, when the string broke.

After the show was over, Stanley Morgan told my mother and father they should be proud of me. I sort of felt embarrassed, especially when my mother said, "We are!" and then kissed me in front of everyone.

While I was packing the puppets away, one of the campers came over to me. He was the chubby red-headed kid who had been in Irwin's group. "Gordie, I want to tell you something," he said, and his lips began to quiver. Before he could say anything else he really started to bawl. He didn't have a handker-chief, and as usual neither did I, so I got a roll of toilet paper from the bathroom. After a lot of nose-blowing and eye-wiping, he was finally able to speak again. "Gordie," he began again, "I was the one who took the puppets apart."

I wasn't mad or anything, and I didn't feel sorry for what I had done to Larry. I just asked him why he did it. He told me that he was really mad at me for letting his bird go—the one he had found and brought into the nature room. I went into a whole thing about how the bird had been able to fly again, and how wrong it would have been to keep it cooped up. He shook his head and said, "I know, Gordie, I'm sorry."

And I said something real dumb like, "Don't ever do it again."

No matter how much I thought about it, I couldn't help but feel glad Larry got his anyway, and I was the one to give it to him. Even if he hadn't ripped the puppets up, he had it coming to him.

The day after the show, my father, mother, Myra and I went to the beach. My mother even went into the water. I splashed at her, and Myra laughed. I looked at Myra, and suddenly it seemed to me that her face didn't seem nearly as bad.

There were just a few days left to the summer, and time was spent closing the camp down. Stanley Morgan told me that if the camp opened up the next year, I could come back. "I'll be fourteen next year," I told him.

At Steiner's we had our annual Labor Day goodbye party. Plastic Chinese lanterns were hung between the bungalows for decoration. And Mrs. Levenson said that she thought it was so pretty that it looked like something out of the movies. Irwin and Myra spent lots of time talking, and I just knew that Myra was going to start writing in her diary again.

Larry came onto the porch of his bungalow wearing a stupid devil mask and holding a flashlight under his chin. Some of the ladies screamed. My mother said, "That reminds me of something, maybe it was a dream I had."

I knew what it reminded my mother of, and it wasn't any dream. I thought about the night of the blackout, and Larry's disappearing act from our porch. I was really happy about the chocolate revenge. Larry came over to me. "Hey Gordie, let's put vinegar in the punch."

"Grow up, Larry, will ya?" I said.

Larry told me to go screw myself and he went over to Harold. When the lanterns were turned off and the last paper cups were picked up, I sat on the porch and thought about how maybe I didn't really understand Larry.

The next day, while Myra and me waited on the porch for my mother to make her final check of the bungalow, Mr. Green, the carpenter from Stuttman's, came by calling, "Here, Puss, here, Puss-puss." When he saw Myra and me he asked us if we had seen a white-and-gray cat around.

"Not recently," said Myra, and we looked at each other.

My mother came out of the bungalow. "Do you know, the closets still smell from that lemon spray Mrs. Kravitz used last year."

We made our way to the train station loaded down with what seemed like more bundles than we had arrived with. And when I told my mother to use my shortcut, she said we'd only end up getting lost and she was in a hurry to get back home.

At home my mother and father had this thing

about how my mother still couldn't believe that Widow Kravitz would play Pokerino on a Saturday and not go to synagogue.

"Maybe she never went to synagogue on Saturday in the first place," said my father. "Or maybe she just got tired of going."

"Or maybe the synagogue closed down," I said, looking at my mother. She knew exactly what I meant. But she didn't have to worry about my father ever knowing about the barbershop one, because me and Myra were sworn to secrecy and we're really good about things like that.

And now that Myra was getting a little better, what difference would it make anyway? Even though there was no *great* improvement in Myra's face, she started seeing Irwin again. And he didn't mind. Because he said it was Myra he liked.

I was soon back at school, and still hating every minute of it. Myra had begun to date Irwin in the city, and he was still bringing her stuffed animal toys. She'd really go crazy—girls are funny that way.

It took some courage, but I asked Phyllis Lavine for a date. I picked her up on a Saturday morning and we ended up taking the train out to the shore. I think I like the beach better in the wintertime any-way. It was a crisp clear day, and the wind whipped around the bungalows. I showed Phyllis which one had been ours. The screen door kept banging from the wind. "It looks haunted," she said.

"I know, but you can take it from me, it isn't!" I said.

We walked along the boardwalk, and everything was boarded up. I told her all about Blue Channel, and the puppets.

When we passed the Texas Bar, I didn't say anything. I just tugged at the small scarf around my neck, the one Lonesome Earl had given me. I'd even read his name in the newspapers. I figured he was doing okay. A sign, *Raided Premises*, hung over the door where the dirty book store had been. "And I never even got one," I said.

"What did you say?" asked Phyllis.

"It was a lot of fun," I said. We held hands and walked toward the end of the boardwalk. A stray dog began to follow us.

"Do you remember how all last year, you used to pretend you were Wolfman?" she said, looking at the dog.

"Yeah, wasn't that silly?" I said.

At the end of the boardwalk there were big cranes and bulldozers in front of Luna Land. A gull, perched on the flagpole at the very top of the glass dome, screamed.

"I hope they don't tear it down," I said.

A cold wind from the ocean swept across the boardwalk, and we kind of huddled together protecting each other.

Format by Kohar Alexanian
Set in 14 pt. Granjon
Composed, printed and bound by
The Haddon Craftsmen, Inc.
Harper & Row, Publishers, Inc.